RECYCLING
HUMANITY

RECYCLING HUMANITY

By Heather Lee Dyer

www.heatherleedyer.com
@HeatherLeeDyer_

Library of Congress Control Number: 2015965851
First Edition May 2015
ISBN 978-0-9962564-0-7 Ebook
ISBN 978-0-9962564-1-4 Paperback

DEDICATION

For my mom who encouraged me to read anything I could get my hands on, and to always reach for the stars.

CHAPTER 1

Orbital Debris

Two hundred thirty-six miles above Earth, reality sinks in as the adrenaline fades from my body.

I push off from the satellite and pull myself along the tether cable, back toward my ship. The nuclear weapons I've found stowed away in this satellite not only are illegal, they complicate my recycling job.

I signal the other ship, using my suit's comm unit. "Kaci to Retriever Ship One I'm leaving the satellite now. There are ten missiles on board, but no radiation leaks detected yet. Her orbit is degrading rapidly, so we need to get the demo team here immediately to take care of the missiles." I disconnect my comm, so I don't have to hear their arguments or questions. I'm freaking out enough being this close to such potential destruction.

Below me, the dying planet is covered with angry, swirling clouds that cover most of its surface. A few clear areas show lifeless brown continents and gray bodies of water. Since I'm one of the first generations born and raised in space, I've never been down to the surface. As I hover weightless, high above abandoned cities, I try to imagine how it used to be beautiful and full of people. But that was before. Before the environment was overcome by pollution, overpopulation, and careless consumption of natural resources. And before the Polymer Bacteria finally finished destroying our home world, killing billions of people over the last couple of decades. Of course, that all happened before I was born, something I've only read about at school, like some distant, disconnected lifetime. Flying in low orbit recycling space junk is the closest I've been.

I tear my attention from the view below and continue toward my ship. I bought the Celeste last year, right after I earned my space pilot's license, a full two years before any of my classmates. Inside my space suit I can feel the calluses on my fingers from all the years of working alongside the mechanics in the bowels of Jupiter Station. It was exhausting work, but it paid very well, enough to buy the Celeste, a used short distance recycling ship, and feed my mom and me. Sometimes Mom kind of checks out mentally, so my after school jobs supported us through her episodes.

Now, I have the perfect high school job; Orbital Debris Recycler. On weekends, I fly in my ship between Earth and the recycler barges to capture old satellites, spent rockets, and any other space junk I can find circling the planet. It's amazing how much stuff we've left up here, millions of pieces of orbital debris, just left, discarded.

Of course, if I lose this satellite, I won't have a job anymore. I'll have to go back to working on barge engines. The time for our migration out of the solar system is coming very soon, and we need all the raw materials we can find before we leave.

I reach my ship and pull myself over to the entrance hatch. Carefully, I disconnect the tether cable, pull the hatch open, and wriggle inside. I take off my helmet and shake out my hair, which has plastered itself to my head. Mom says my dark brown, annoyingly straight hair and my warm skin tones come from my father. She always says this with tears in her beautiful blue eyes, since we lost him when I was a little girl. Some days I wonder if we lost more than just my father.

I pull off my suit, groaning as I realize it's going to need to be cleaned when I get back. Sweating in this suit for the last eight hours means I probably look pretty scary. I pause, trying to remember when my last sani-shower was. I've been so busy this weekend that I seriously doubt it was anytime recent.

I bring my attention back to the problem outside. Usually, after stripping everything useful from inside the satellite, I would drop to a lower orbit to allow a retriever ship to grab it, and tow the space junk to the recycler barges. There, they would weigh it, and I would split the profits with the retriever team. Unfortunately, my discovery of the nuclear weapons has complicated a normally simple job.

I pull myself over to the main control console, a blinking red light alerting me to a message. The demo team is still a good twenty minutes from my location. I check the satellite's orbit and trajectory, and cringe. Crap. It's headed toward the only spot on the whole planet that still has human inhabitants. I know from the news vid feeds, that old Seattle, in the North American continent, is where the Compound is located. The

Compound protects the scientists who are still working to complete the Eugenesis Project before they, too, have to leave Earth and join the migration out of our solar system.

I don't really have any sort of personal attachment to the planet below, but this is my job. Which I need desperately. Most importantly, I need to show Jupiter Command that I'm not only the best pilot they have, of any age, but that I'm more than capable of handling any situation thrown at me. I've worked hard toward my goal of becoming the first female pilot on one of the super fast scout ships. I not only need to keep my job, I need that promotion as well. Besides finally getting the job I've always wanted to do my whole life, I know that my mom is counting on me.

The comm crackles, and I see that it is Devon Durrant, who happens to be the second youngest certified pilot, as well as the son of the commander of Jupiter Station. Fabulous. This day truly can get even worse. Devon's always resented that I earned my certification before him, and I continue to have better grades than him. High school sucks. I sigh, steady myself mentally, and answer him. "Yes, Devon."

"Kaci, what are you doing over there? Trying to get yourself busted down to working on the garbage barges?" As he laughs at his own joke, I can hear his friends, who I have named the Misfits, snorting with laughter in the background. I roll my eyes so hard I give myself a headache.

Devon owns one of the largest retriever class ships. It's capable of towing several of these satellites back to the barges at one time, but it takes a crew of at least four to manage. Devon is handsome, powerful, and rich. He's the whole package. Unfortunately, he knows it, and has always tended to push the limits, break the rules, and pick on anyone he sees as weaker than him. Usually, that person is me. Although annoying to be the object of his bullying, it has made me stronger, and more competitive. I wasn't going to let him make me a victim. He has always been in all my flight and physical training classes; my biggest competition, and my biggest problem. The Misfits are like ugly growths on Devon's side; they go everywhere together, and pick on me together. I can't escape their torment, especially now that we're on the same recycling team.

I swallow a nasty retort, take a deep breath, and explain my situation in as few words as possible.

He doesn't say anything.

"So, are you going to help me out here, Devon? We need to get those missiles out and disarmed." Having to ask him for help, makes me sick to my stomach, but I don't have a choice.

After another long pause, he finally answers. "Since the demo team won't get here in time, I guess I'll have to save the day."

I imagine the smirk on his face, enjoying my discomfort and the fact that I need him. He moves his ship closer to the satellite.

"All right! Let's try to catch this satellite before it gets sucked out of orbit. Hang on Kaci, and watch a real pilot work!" He cuts the comm, leaving me in silence once again, and slides his ship into the orbit below.

Devon's ship looks like a many-segmented beetle, the black kind that scurries around the plants in the greenhouse back at Jupiter Station. The bridge of his ship makes up the head of the beetle, the cargo area the body, and the many pieces of recycled junk attached around the hull look like crazy insect legs.

The traction arms attached at the back end of his ship swing out and line up with the dead satellite. On my readouts, I see that the demo team is still too far out of range. I sigh again and move closer to Devon's ship, getting ready to help if necessary. If the demo team doesn't get here soon, we're left with two options. One, I will have to transfer the nukes into my storage bay, and then Devon can take the satellite to the barge. I don't like that idea, since my ship doesn't have strong enough radiation shielding. It makes me nervous thinking of such dangerous weapons inside my ship. Our second option is to use Devon's ship to tow the whole satellite to the demo team for disarming. Unfortunately, his ship uses strong electromagnetic energy in order to attach the space junk to his ship's outer hull. This virtually fries any electrical systems left aboard the space junk, which is usually acceptable. But not in this situation, since we don't know if it will trigger the nukes. Both options have me a nervous wreck.

Another blinking light on my console alerts me to some space debris drifting nearby. I quickly open the comm, "Devon, that hunk of junk is heading for what looks like an expended rocket booster. Can you pull the satellite up farther into orbit, without setting off the nukes?" My hands are clammy and my heart is racing. Being this close to live nukes makes me wonder if any size of collision with the satellite would set them off.

Devon's deep voice sounds through the comm. "I see it, I see it! I'm still trying to latch on to the satellite without puncturing its hull. I'd rather not blow up my ship." Calm, cool Devon sounds a bit nervous. Not good.

Devon dodges the debris, just barely, and finally gets the satellite stabilized between the mechanical arms. Unfortunately, this takes his ship lower into the planet's atmosphere, and they get caught in the gravity well. The planet is drawing him down.

"Devon? What's going on over there?"

"I'm trying to use my side thrusters to get back up to orbit. The nukes are too close to my main engine."

This is not going well. I study the readings on the control panel and try to remember all my emergency training. We did go through sims where we had to land on Earth, but we've never practiced it in real life.

"Kaci, I'm too low. We can't get free without lighting up the nukes." Devon sounds close to panic now.

"Devon, looks like the only option now is to land on Earth. Then, we can wait for the demo team down there."

"No, Kaci, I've never done an Earth landing. None of us have."

"I know, but there isn't any other choice. You can do this. I'll be right behind you." I wait, hoping he will listen to me and not light his engines. I've got to keep him calm.

"Okay. Just like the sims, right? I'll head for the Compound, since that's probably the only safe place to land."

"Just remember our training, Devon, and you'll be fine. See you down there." I prepare my ship to enter the atmosphere and follow Devon down toward the last place in the universe I ever thought I'd be going to.

He descends below me, his ship engulfed quickly in the gray swirling clouds. I leave another message for the demo team, letting them know our intended location. I anxiously watch my screens as my ship shudders and lurches as I fall toward Earth.

CHAPTER 2

Earth

I trust my training and my ship to handle the stormy atmosphere as I program in a landing course near where Devon and the satellite are headed. The Celeste is a small ship, but she handles well. I've made several Lunar landings with her, but I have no idea what to expect below the clouds here on Earth.

My view screens go dark as I enter the dense clouds. I have to rely completely on my ship's computers.

I try to reach the other ship. "Devon, how are you doing? Can you hear me?"

No response. I'm not sure if he's just out of comm range or if our comms don't work in these clouds. If you had told me years ago that I would be landing on Earth, following a tin can full of dangerous nuclear weapons, and worrying about the biggest bully on Jupiter Station, I would have laughed until I peed myself. I'm sure not laughing now.

The comm crackles, and I barely hear Devon's voice, but at least I know he's still alive.

"It's going to be close, Kaci. I'm not sure about this landing. I hope the impact will not set off your stupid nukes." Yep. He's nervous, and still annoying.

"I'm right behind you, Devon. You're doing fine. Just keep those nukes from jarring and remember the procedures for landing in gravity."

No human these days would ever have created or kept anything so destructive as nuclear weapons. We have learned to be peaceful, and thankful for what little we have left of our civilization. These nukes are from a long time ago.

Nowadays, scientists and engineers use their knowledge and technology to build habitat ships for all the survivors from Earth. They have already recycled everything useful from down on the planet. Now we're just cleaning up the space junk.

The comm crackles but then goes silent as Devon's ship falls from range of my sensors. I switch frequencies to offset the magnetic activity, trying to keep contact with his ship. I track his ship to the northern most part of former Washington State. Good, at least he's heading in the right direction. The clouds surrounding us have turned black and swirling, and are filled with energy. My little ship is knocked around, but she stays on course. Minutes tick by. I imagine Devon crashing, and the nukes exploding. I'm not sure why I care so much, but at this moment my stomach is in knots worrying about him. Unbelievable, Kaci! Years of imagining Devon being flushed out of an airlock or burned up in a fiery crash, and now here I am worried he won't survive. The station psych would love this.

Finally, the Celeste breaks through the clouds, and Devon's ship comes into view. It looks to me like he's going in too fast, too low. I hold my breath as he skims over dead and fallen forests, remnants of old structures, and mountains of dirt as far as the eye can see. Off to my left I see the Compound, giant metal structures pummeled by wind and dirt. A fence so large it seems almost as tall as the buildings, surrounds it, protecting its inhabitants. I wonder what this fortress of a fence was built for, since there is nothing and nobody else down there.

My attention goes back to where Devon's ship is headed toward the side of a small mountain. At least he's not going to take out the Compound.

His landing is not at all graceful. In a cloud of spraying dirt, he lands halfway buried at the foot of the mountain. No explosions or smoke though. Now it's my turn.

Wanting to show Devon I can do this better than him, too, I calculate carefully so my landing barely disturbs any of the dry barren landscape. I settle the Celeste down gently, just a few meters from Devon's ship. I flip the switches to open the hatch, and hurry to untangle myself from the harness and bio interfaces. I scramble out and immediately stumble for several steps, almost doing a face plant. Although I know better, the difference in gravity has caught me by surprise. Jupiter Station does have artificial gravity, but it must not be the same as Earth's gravity. I feel heavy and slow, like I'm walking through water.

I cover the distance between the two ships as quickly as I can. I see that Devon's hatch is partway open, near where the beetle head would connect with its body. I see scratches and shallow gouges in the hull, and I feel sick as I trudge toward the ship.

I realize I have been holding my breath, so I stop and take a few steadying breaths. I can't let them see that I'm worried.

I glance past where the grapplers still cradle the ugly satellite. It looks like it's still in one piece. I make a mental checklist as I walk: I need to check the nukes and the satellite, and then figure out how to get them back up to the recycle barges. The barges are built with shielding that can handle the uranium in the weapons as long as we disarm them before delivery. Guess I need to add that to my checklist: figure out how to disarm the missiles. Hopefully, someone on the demo team can walk us through it.

The demo team! I wonder if they are on their way still, or do they assume we are all dead? Would they follow us planet-side as we requested, or would they wait in orbit? I feel my brain start to freeze up. Again, I have to remind myself to breathe and stay calm. I can do this. If I can fight my way through pilot school by age seventeen, I can handle this. First, I need to make sure Devon and the Misfits are still alive. Then I can worry about the rest.

I reach Devon's ship and find that the hatch lid has been twisted slightly in the crash, and is stuck halfway open.

I yell into the small opening. "Devon! Are you okay?" I hear some movement inside. Good, that means someone is alive.

Devon finally answers from within. "Kaci! It's good to hear your voice! I might have broken my wrist, and the guys are a bit banged up. What about the nukes? Did I damage the satellite? You're okay? Did you get injured? How's your ship?"

He's rambling and actually sounds worried. Not being used to this side of Devon, I am speechless. Is he truly concerned about me, or does he have a concussion? I shake myself mentally. I don't have time to think about this right now. There are more important issues to deal with.

My voice cracks a bit as I answer him. "My ship is fine, and yours looks like it took a bit of damage, but nothing we can't fix. I think the nukes are all right for now. Nothing is sizzling or blowing up, but we need to take a closer look at them. Can you get out of there?" My relief that Devon is alive fades quickly, as I am overwhelmed by the enormity of the situation. I sit down hard on the ground, and lean back against his ship. Another thought crosses my mind. "Devon, what about the bacteria that destroyed everything down here? Is it still alive? Do you think it will hurt our ships?" I think I've let his panic get to me.

Devon taps on the ship to get my attention. "Let's take this one step at a time. You go check on the nukes, while I find a way out of here. I think I can pry this door the rest of the way open, I just need to go get some tools. Come back and let me know how bad the damage is."

I hear him shuffling away from the hatch, his ship creaking with the movement. I notice he didn't say anything about the bacteria. Great.

I get up and slowly walk around the back of his ship. A loud noise in the distance startles me, and I look up. I shield my eyes from the brightness. Strange that it can be so light down here, when the skies are all covered with clouds. I scan the area looking for the source of the noise, which sounds like a cross between the giant greenhouse fans on Jupiter Station, and a small engine on overload.

I eventually spot a low flying small ship heading toward us. Disappointed, I realize it's not the demo team. It must be a hovercraft from the Compound. I figure it will take some time to reach us, so I continue toward the satellite.

I carefully approach it, looking for the main access opening. It seems like such a long time since I was just jumping out of this thing into the blackness of space above us.

Already I can tell something is wrong. The sides of the satellite have hairline cracks running along the sides. Stress fractures. Satellites are not built strong like space ships. In space, satellites usually only need to deflect a small meteorite or two. They weren't designed to re-enter Earth's atmosphere, let alone crash on Earth. The only reason this one made it this far is because it was protected by the force field of Devon's ship.

I open the hatch carefully, and get hit by screaming alarms and flashing lights. I have no idea what they are trying to tell me, but I doubt that it's anything good.

I replace the hatch, and make my way back to Devon's ship. Working with nuclear weapons definitely was not in my course load. I need to come up with Plan B.

CHAPTER 3

Devon

Devon has gotten the hatch off its hinges, and the rest of the Misfits are just climbing out. "Are you guys all right?" I ask.

A high nasally voice answers me. "Of course we are. We aren't weak little girls." Marsh. A jerk even in a bad situation. With an annoying voice like that and a personality to match, I'm surprised he has any friends, let alone Devon Durrant. I guess that's one benefit of being one of Devon's friends, automatic popularity.

Marsh has cut the side of his head, and blood is trickling through his stringy black hair. I smile in satisfaction. "Well,

Marsh, at least I don't have a scratch on me, and you look like you forgot to tighten your helmet again." His helmet dangles from the back of his space suit, and looks like it took quite a beating.

Marsh sits down hard on the ground. "Whatever, Kaci. We wouldn't be stranded on this deserted planet if you'd done your job properly."

Before I can open my mouth in response, Devon steps in between Marsh and me. "Calm down, both of you. None of us knew there were nukes still in that satellite. Let's just concentrate on fixing this problem. Marsh, you go get the emergency kit and get that head wound to stop bleeding. Also have Lewis make sure Alex is okay. Alex was in the back section working the mechanical arm controls when we landed."

Devon turns to me, grabs my hand, and pulls me toward the satellite. "Let's see what we're dealing with."

Surprised, I look down at our clasped hands, but I don't pull mine back. I allow him to steer us toward the satellite, shocked at the sudden intimate touch.

As we walk, I can see Devon is struggling with the heavy gravity as well. Good. It's not just me.

"So Kaci, what exactly did you see? Do you think the nukes are okay?" He looks at me with those wicked blue eyes. Along with being drop-dead gorgeous, he was blessed with long, dark eyelashes that any girl would kill to have. My hand, still in his, feels like it's on fire. I drop my gaze away from him and stare at my shoes.

I struggle to get my mind back on what's at stake here. "No, I don't think they're okay. I think the nukes are going to be a problem, and soon. The satellite has structural damage, and there are alarms going off inside. We really need the demo team. We can't do this by ourselves. We don't have the training." I'm trying hard not to sound scared, but I'm sure Devon can tell I'm nervous about the situation.

He squeezes my hand. "I'm sure we'll figure out something, Kaci. You helped me keep calm through my panicked landing. And we're safe so far."

Somehow, that's not very reassuring to me.

We reach the satellite, and Devon lets go of my hand. He walks around the perimeter, opening compartments and flipping switches. Curious, I ask him, "How is it that you know so much about these old satellites? I only knew where to find the main entrance. I thought your specialty was recycle ships, not old Earth technology?"

He looks back at me with that smile, that one that always gets him out of trouble. "My father studied Earth history. In his position, he has access to all of the Earth and space history archives. Some of it's actually pretty interesting. He's always telling me that it's important to know where we have been in order to see where we need to go. Something about not making the same mistakes over and over. That's why he makes such a good commander. So, I've been studying along with him. He thinks I might make a good commander someday." His smile gets wider. I just roll my eyes in response. "I especially like learning about all the old technology, like this satellite here." He pats the metal beside him. That killer smile, and his passion as he talks, takes my breath away. I can see why the girls at school think he's so wonderful, and follow him around like lost little puppies.

I take a step back from him.

I pretend to study a crack on the portion of satellite in front of me. "Well, I really don't know the commander that well, but he sounds like a great father." Waves of sorrow and jealousy wash over me. I turn away so Devon can't see the emotions that I'm struggling with. It's strange for me to be talking to Devon at all, especially on such a personal level. Right now he doesn't seem like the egocentric bully I have faced all these years.

Devon steps close to me until I'm forced to look at him. He's studying my face and frowns. I try concentrating on making my face blank, emotionless.

Amazingly, he doesn't take advantage of my weakness. He doesn't even comment on the tears that are threatening to spill over in my eyes. He just continues on, holding my stare. "Something else I learned about these kind of satellites. They were made before the Polymer Bacteria. So, unlike our ships, they might still have plastic components. That could be really bad if the plastic-destroying bacteria is still active down here. Another reason the demo team needs to hurry."

The Polymer Bacteria outbreak in the 2020s had destroyed everything made of any type of plastic. In the beginning, this bacterium had been designed to dissolve the billions of tons of plastics overflowing the world's landfills, treatment plants, and factories. If it had worked, it would have helped solve the pollution problems that were already ruining Earth's fragile environment. But the bacteria soon mutated to destroy other manmade materials, and it couldn't be contained. It infiltrated urban and isolated areas equally, through water supplies and eventually even became airborne. Plastics and other man-made polymers were an integral part of everything in the 2020s; air and water purification components, storage containers, ground and air transportation parts, materials in building houses and buildings, everyday household items, weapons, even clothing contained some sort of polymer or another. Buildings and structures crumbled. Machinery and transportation soon ceased as important parts dissolved before everyone's eyes. It all happened quicker than they could come up with a solution. Civilization lost more than half of its food storage, since plastic containers were the preferred method of long term storage. Food production couldn't keep up with the immediate demands of the masses of people worldwide. Billions of lives were lost in that first year after the outbreak due to starvation, exposure, dehydration.

I force myself to move away from Devon and his mesmerizing eyes and start toward my ship. "Right. Let's get back to the Celeste to try to radio the demo team," I say over my shoulder. What is the matter with me? I've never been attracted to Devon. Get a grip, Kaci. He's the same boy you've competed alongside all these years.

I climb into the Celeste, and without looking, know that Devon is still right behind me. Ignoring him, I sit in my pilot's chair and push the comm button. "Demo team delta. Can you hear us? We need you to meet us at these coordinates for extraction of nuclear weapons. Demo team?" I'm answered only by the crackling of an empty connection.

Turning around, I find Devon sitting down next to me in the copilot's chair. He looks like he belongs here in my ship. For some reason this irritates me a tiny bit. He runs his hand over the console in front of him, back and forth, deep in thought. I recognize this as a habit he's had since he was little. Growing up, I always thought it was a sign of greedy possessiveness, as if he just touched everything, it would then be his. Now, as I look closely at the expression on his face, I see that it might just be a nervous habit. To clear his head while he's thinking.

I look away, conscious of how close we are in this small space. "Now what, Devon? I don't think they can hear us through the storm above. My ship is fine, I landed without breaking anything." I give him a hint of a smile. "Maybe we should take off, and get above the cloud cover to signal them?"

Devon turns and leans closer toward me. He looks worried. "I don't know, Kaci. The satellite doesn't look so good. Even though I know a bit about satellite technology, I don't know anything about dealing with the weapons. Those we need to do something about very soon. The Compound isn't far from here, so all those people are in danger as well, if the weapons detonate. I don't think we have time to go looking for the demo team."

I look at the console that shows our location on the planet. "You're right. I think we're too close to the Compound. The Project is important to our leaders." I don't say it out loud, but I don't really care if Earth is healed or not. It has never been my home. All I want to do right now is fire up my ship, and get back to the comfort of space. That's where all the people are anyway, not on this planet that I can't do anything for.

The nukes do create a problem though. If they go off now, they would not only destroy us, but the Project as well.

Devon surprises me by reaching over, and taking both of my hands in his. I was so deep in thought about Earth and the nukes, I had forgotten he was so close. "Kaci, even though this is a pretty sucky situation, I know we'll get out of this somehow. I'm glad we're stranded here together. All these years I've watched how quickly you learn, and how strong of a competitor you are. With both of us working on this problem, I know we can figure out something." Devon drops his gaze to the floor. "And I know it's bad timing, but I want to tell you I'm sorry for all the meanness in the past. I felt threatened by always coming in second place to you."

My mind tries to come up with some kind of mean response, deserving of all those years of grief, but I can't think of anything to say. I'm speechless. He looks back up at me, and his blue eyes capture my gaze. I can't look away, and

I haven't even pulled my hands back. Being this close to him makes all the bad times seem so very far away. I wonder if he's just being nice because we are stranded on this planet and about to possibly die? Or does he truly regret the past?

"Devon..." As my mind struggles for something to say, I hear the hovercraft approaching. Devon hears it too. The moment is broke, and Devon releases my hands. We scramble outside.

In a cloud of dust, a hovercraft glides toward us. I glance sideways at Devon and wonder what just happened between us? In the midst of all this chaos, there was a sense of some sort of connection. Could this be a start of a friendship, or even something more? I stand close to Devon, covering my eyes as the hovercraft sprays us with dirt. I watch it land awkwardly in the sand, and I wonder how I let my life get so complicated.

CHAPTER 4

Abishai

The hovercraft finally settles into the dirt way too close to my ship, which ignites my temper. There is nothing but sand and dirt as far as the eye can see, and this pilot chooses to land practically on top of my ship. I've just gone through a horrible storm, safely landing my ship for the first time in gravity, and now this pilot threatens to damage the Celeste. In my head, I've got a few choice words for these people.

I step forward as the dust settles down and get our first glimpse of the two people that emerge from the hovercraft. An older gentleman gets out first, and I recognize him immediately. All the colorful words I've come up with get stuck in my throat. This man is the reason it is so important to get the nukes out of here. He is Dr. Kincaid, the creator of the Eugenesis Project. He's dubbed the savior of the future of Earth, a hero to all the humans that have survived the last few decades of losing their planet.

But here, in person, he's just an old, pasty pale, balding man, whose murky gray eyes are looking around at our ships angrily. I should've expected him to be upset at us landing so close to the Compound, but right now I feel that I'm the one who should be angry.

I strain to look behind him as I wonder what other surprises await us. The other person steps out of the hovercraft, and my pulse quickens as he turns his face toward me. I look into the brightest, clearest green eyes I've ever seen. His face is framed by tight, curly brown hair, and mocha brown skin. While Devon is handsome, this boy, maybe a year older than me, is exotically gorgeous in comparison. Stunned, all I can think of at this moment is how awful I must look. I've just crawled out of a sweaty space suit, crash landed on a dusty planet, and I'm stumbling around like a complete idiot in this heavy gravity. This is not the way to make a good impression. I look down at my rumpled and dirty suit and frown.

My self-incrimination is interrupted by Green Eyes, who has walked up to us and stands right before me, uncomfortably close. He holds out his hand to me. "I am Abishai, and this is my father, Dr. Kincaid." He nods in the direction of the older man, who has stopped several feet behind him. Abishai's speech is formal, making him sound more mature than his age.

I look over and see Dr. Kincaid still wears an angry expression. Devon steps forward to shake Dr. Kincaid's hand, but I keep my arms pinned to my sides. I glance over at the hovercraft, then back at Abishai. "You almost took out my ship, landing your hunk of junk too close." The words come out sounding harsher than I intend. Smooth, Kaci. Verbal communication is not a strong point of mine. Especially around guys. My nerves tend to remove my verbal filter, creating awkward social situations.

Abishai drops his hand in midair and takes a step back from me, as if stung physically by my harsh words. "I am sorry. I do not get to fly much and especially not out here to rescue people who have crashed so close to our Compound." Although his tone sounds angry, I see a flash of humor cross his face. He's staring at me, watching for a reaction.

Out of the corner of my eye, I see Devon having a hard time keeping a straight face. Great. I always tend to say the wrong thing, especially when I'm flustered. Before Devon can enjoy this too much, I awkwardly apologize to Abishai and Dr. Kincaid and briefly explain our situation. I quickly excuse myself, letting Devon fill in the rest of the story.

With my cheeks burning, I duck into the Celeste. I sink into my seat, and bang my forehead repeatedly on the console. When will I ever to be able to talk to a guy without coming across like sandpaper? Even though I'm proud of how hard I've worked to get my flight certification, sometimes I envy the other girls my age. While I was training in the simulators or studying how to fix a broken landing booster, the other girls were getting their nails and makeup done for dates. They always look beautiful and perfect, all the time. They know all the right things to say to guys. I'm lucky to remember a sani-shower and to pull a brush through my hair.

A sharp knock startles me out of my pity party, and I straighten up. In the hatchway stands Abishai. I rub the spot on my forehead where I'm sure there's a traitorous red mark.

Embarrassed, I turn back around and push the comm button. "Demo team delta, Kaci here. Can you hear me, delta?" Abishai has stepped inside, and is now calmly leaning against the co-pilot's chair.

The same spot, not twenty minutes ago, Devon was just sitting holding my hands. I try to push those thoughts of Devon to the back of my mind and ignore Abishai, who is standing so close. Well, I try to ignore him. "Demo team delta, please respond. We are in need of help at our location." I'm answered with loud crackling. Could this day get any worse?

Abishai waits patiently, until I finally look up from the console. He doesn't acknowledge my display of frustration, but instead says, "Not only did you and your boyfriend interrupt our work, put us in danger with the nuclear weapons, but you have also landed on one of my project drone transmitters. It is broken beyond repair." His voice is soft spoken, and his speech is still politely formal, but his eyes have a look of controlled anger.

At this point I don't know if he is amused by the situation, or if he's really angry, so I choose to go on the defensive. "Actually, Devon is not my boyfriend, and we did not crush your transmitter on purpose. We were kind of busy just trying to stay alive. Devon did the best he could to land safely with the cargo. We could've just let the satellite fall and explode all over your precious Compound. At least that way, I wouldn't be stranded down here on this planet." I get up and try to push past Abishai. He grabs my arm gently but firmly, and turns me to face him. I freeze. Up close he doesn't look angry anymore, just worried. Those eyes, though, they have me mesmerized.

For the second time in a matter of minutes, I feel the need to apologize.

"I'm sorry. I'm better with ships than people. It's been a very long day." I try to escape his grasp, but he has a solid grip on me, so I continue, "I can try to fix your transmitter, but first we need to deal with the nukes, or none of us will survive, and your Project will be worthless."

He doesn't drop his gaze from mine. "I will have my father head back to the Compound to use the Sat comm to reach your demo team." He smiles. "Will that help?"

Between his gorgeous green eyes, his warm hand on my arm, and that killer smile, he's made me feel all warm inside, and speechless. I just dumbly smile back. Way to take charge of the situation, Kaci. I mentally shake my head in frustration at myself.

Abishai continues, "In the meantime, Kaci, I can take a look at those nukes, and see if I can figure out how to disarm them. I am pretty good with electronics. I helped design the whole drone system for the Project. Even though this satellite was probably made before either of us was born, I still might be able to help." He quickly adds, "At least until your team gets here, of course."

I finally find my voice. "Fine. Let's see what you can do with these nukes." He releases his grasp, and I step out the hatch. I walk as quickly as I can, without looking back to see if he's following.

I walk over to where things seem to be a little tense between Devon and Dr. Kincaid. I look at Devon, but he just shrugs his shoulders and clenches his jaw. Not a good sign. Devon is the kind of person who can win anyone over, and everyone loves him. Apparently Abishai's father is the rare exception. I'm about to ask what is going on, when Abishai comes up behind me and joins us.

Abishai stops with his shoulder touching mine, and smiles at me, and then nods at Devon. I freeze and try to keep my

25

face neutral. He pulls his father to the side and has a whispered conversation with him. My face flushes warm, and I don't even want to look at Devon. I would prefer scrubbing filters in the sewer plant than having to deal with this awkward situation. This is exactly why I don't date, or even socialize, really. I'm not good at it.

I finally take a peek at Devon. He's still tense, and is keeping a close eye on Abishai and Dr. Kincaid. Good, he hasn't noticed my embarrassment. I try to fill in the awkward silence by asking about his crew. He answers me without turning his head. "Alex ended up getting thrown around quite a bit. I think he might have a broken leg. We need to get him off this planet and back to Jupiter Station, so the docs can fix him up." We watch as Abishai gestures with his hands as he speaks to his father. Dr. Kincaid looks angry, but he seems to be listening.

Devon turns to face me. "Marsh will be fine, he has a hard head, as you know." All his tenseness is starting to fade away. I think he's amused by the conflict between Abishai and his father. Devon lifts his arm to show me the white temp cast. "We found a compression cast for my wrist. This should do until I get back." Devon steps closer to me and places his good arm protectively around my shoulder. He clutches his injured wrist to his chest. "Were you able to reach the demo team, Kaci?"

I don't answer right away, being very aware of his arm draped around me. Dr. Kincaid and Abishai finish their conversation, and Dr. Kincaid turns and hurries off to the hovercraft. He gets in and leaves in a cloud of dust. Abishai walks back over to us and stands right in front of Devon and me.

My face flushes again, as I feel Devon's arm weighing down on me. I answer Devon's earlier question. "No, the team still didn't respond." I look over at Abishai, certain my face is red as a tomato. "Abishai's father is going to use his Sat comm to reach our team. With his technology he should be able to get through this storm. Right, Abishai?"

Abishai nods, but doesn't say anything.

I look back and forth between Abishai and Devon and feel trapped. I may be naive socially, but I haven't gotten this far in life only to be placed in the middle of high school posturing when there are more important issues going on down here. I fall back into my old survival instincts, and duck out from under Devon's arm, turn and walk away without a word to either one of them. Let them deal with the tension without me.

CHAPTER 5

Satellite

I head toward the satellite, trying to push the situation with Devon and Abishai out of my mind. I need to concentrate on what I learned from my electrical classes. Unfortunately, the information I can recall is very limited, since we have technology that has made wiring such as in this satellite obsolete.

I take a quick detour back to my ship and grab my portable toolbox. When I reach the satellite, I find Abishai already there, opening the main hatch. Devon is nowhere in sight. Good. I can only handle one of them at a time. I walk around to the other side of the satellite, and squat down to look for the cover to the power panel. Maybe if I can cut the main power, the missiles won't have enough juice for them to power up. I'm not sure, but I need to do something. The familiarity of working with my tools again calms me.

Suddenly, Abishai is standing over me. It surprises me, and I lose my balance. I sit down hard in the dirt. Abishai crouches down, trying hard to hold back a smile. "Are you all right? I did not mean to scare you."

"Crap! Don't sneak up on me like that!"

"I was making enough noise to wake up the dead, Kaci. I was just coming to see if you found the main power panel." He picks up the tool I dropped, and cracks a smile. "Is there something wrong? You seem jumpy."

His smile makes me hold back any wisecrack I was going to come up with. Instead I say, "No, nothing's wrong. Well, other than the obvious situation we are in. I was just—" Struggling a bit, I stand up. I dust myself off and try to regain my composure. "I was just concentrating."

"Sure, I understand." Between his closeness to me and his smile that could melt chocolate, my heart skips a beat. He hands me back my tool, his fingers brushing mine. "I was just coming over to ask you for some help. Once the power is cut from out here, there's a backup inside we'll need to cut as well. I'll need your assistance and your tools to get to that one, while I try to take care of the nuclear weapons." His gaze travels from my eyes down to my toolbox. "Looks like you're pretty good with tools."

I smile up at him. "Thanks. I am." I try again to wipe the dirt off my pants.

I finish unbolting the protective cover to expose the power switches. "Ready for me to throw these switches? It will take a few minutes for all the power to drain out of the main capacitors."

He checks his watch. "Yes, go ahead."

I flip all the switches to the off position, and we make our way quickly to the other side of the satellite. Abishai is much more graceful in this gravity. He has the main entry hatch open by the time I catch up to him. I push my toolbox in first, and then hoist myself through. Abishai follows. The inside is only about three meters wide. The ceiling is low, so Abishai has to crouch down a bit, but I don't have a problem. One benefit of being short.

The blinking lights and alarms have been joined by several other screeching warning bells. I cover my ears and yell over to Abishai, "Can you turn those off?"

He steps over to one side of the room and pushes some buttons, and the sounds cease, although the lights still continue to flash. "Better?" Again that smile.

"Yes, thanks." I look around and see that the nukes are strapped in around three sides of the room. The impact has shifted some of them slightly. "So, where is that secondary power?"

Before he can answer, I notice a slight warm draft. "Uh, Abishai. Where is that heat coming from?" Now I'm getting nervous. When you live in space, you become very aware of what radiation can do to the body.

Abishai looks worried as well. He frowns as he pokes around the wires and switches along one wall. "The cooling fans and air scrubbers must have been damaged in the crash. The secondary power system should have kept those going. I hope your demo team gets here soon. In the meantime, I'll see if I can buy us some time." He starts tearing off panel covers from the main console. I notice that he is also pretty good with tools. He moves around in this small place like he has been doing this his whole life. I enjoy watching him work, and take the opportunity while he's concentrating, to study his features. The heavier gravity has made him muscular, and well-toned. Not typical of scientists stuck in a lab all day.

I hear a whooshing sound, and feel a cold breeze blowing from the vents above and below us. Relief floods over me. "Nice! Looks like you have the fans back on line!"

"It's just temporary. It should help keep them cool for an hour or so. Now, we just need to check if the weapons themselves were damaged." He wipes perspiration off his forehead. His curls are stuck to his forehead, and his face is flushed. I wonder how much radiation we've already been exposed to.

Shouts come from outside, and I hear a loud noise from above. Abishai and I scramble out of the satellite. Devon and Marsh are doing a happy dance on the other side of our ships. The demo team must be here. I smile at their antics. Even in this scary, crappy situation, we are still teenagers. Laughing along with them, I look up in the sky and see the large ship descending in the distance. Across the landscape, I also see the hovercraft coming back toward us.

I take a step away from the ship to join the others, and feel my head spinning. Just as I feel myself falling, Abishai catches me in his strong arms. I look up at him and say, "Sorry, I'm still not used to the extra gravity." I try to wiggle out of his embrace, but he has his arm firmly around my waist. I stop struggling. My skin tingles from his touch.

His forehead creases with concern. "Kaci, you know it's not the gravity." I see that he's still sweating. His arms holding me up are warm, too warm.

Weakly, I say, "Crap, we were exposed to too much radiation, weren't we?" He stands me up slowly, and I reluctantly step out of his arms.

"Yes, I believe the radiation leak was worse than I first thought." He looks away, toward the approaching hovercraft.

"We have doctors at the Compound that can help. Radiation sickness is common to anyone who spends any time out here. There's not much protection from the sun anymore." He sounds sad, and maybe a little bitter. This has been his home, and his whole world changed right before him while he was growing up, while I was safe up on Jupiter Station, going to school and flying among the stars. I didn't have to see the planet dying in front of me like he did.

"I'm sorry, Abishai. I guess I never really thought how it would be like living down here, while all this was going on." Now that I see the devastation, the dead ecosystem, destroyed infrastructure, abandoned land, for myself, I truly feel for humanity's loss. And it makes me sad seeing how it has affected Abishai, even though I haven't known him long. "I've always lived on Jupiter Station, but my mom's family actually lived in an area not too far from here, in what they use to call Idaho. My father's family lived on the island of Japan, before the bacteria hit that side of the world."

I stand just a few feet away from Abishai, but I feel like we are worlds apart. We have lived such different lives, had such different experiences. I notice fondness in his eyes as he surveys the landscape around us. All I see is dirt and dying trees, but he looks like he sees what used to be, before it was all destroyed.

The hovercraft lands near my ship again, capturing Abishai's attention. We watch as people climb out. Abishai's father didn't come back, but there are technicians and medics that have come to help us. The demo team has landed as well, and Abishai walks over to join them at the satellite.

I find Devon working in his ship. "You're not helping the demo team?" I ask. He smiles at me as I climb aboard. I carefully sit down next to him, trying not to lose my balance again.

"No, they have everything under control. I need to make sure my ship will get me home. I think I have most of the systems up and running." He gestures outside. "As long as I don't have to tow that stupid satellite up, I should be able to get through the atmosphere and away from here." Even in his exhausted state and his hair plastered to his head with sweat, he's still quite handsome. His blue eyes look me over with concern. "How are you, Kaci? You look flushed. Radiation sickness, or just glad to see me?" He attempts a weak smile.

I'm not used to him being nice, so it takes me a moment to reply. I nod, trying to decide if I missed noticing this side of Devon before, or if he just hid it well over the years. "Yes, the cooling fans were damaged. Radiation escaped into the main compartment before we got the fan system fixed. Abishai and I were both exposed. It's not too bad yet, and the Compound has doctors trained to treat radiation poisoning." I look down, nervous to be this close to Devon again. Strange how just days ago I wouldn't have thought about Devon this way at all. I wonder if this nice Devon will disappear once we leave Earth; I'm surprised I even care.

With his good hand, Devon reaches out and gently pulls my chin up, so I'm looking directly at him. "Can't you just come back with us and get treated by the doctors on Jupiter Station?" Devon's intense blue eyes seem to show concern for me. Or is it jealousy? Since I haven't dealt with this kind of attention from a boy before, I'm not quite sure what to think. "My ship should be ready soon, you could just ride back with me. We could have Lewis fly your ship back."

I break away from his grasp abruptly. "There's no way I'm going to let Lewis touch the Celeste!" With the sudden movement, my head starts spinning again. "Besides, the quicker I get treatment, the less side effects I'll have, and the sooner I can get back to flying. I don't want to be on this planet any longer either. I just can't wait that long to get treated. I'm getting lightheaded already."

Devon's face clouds over, and I can almost see him erecting a wall between us. "Yes, I know, I understand, Kaci. It makes sense. Radiation sickness can be deadly, and we also really need to get your load to the recycler." He leans away from me, breaking eye contact. "I just don't like leaving you down here with them." Even though he has tried to move away from me, we are still just inches from one another in this small space. After a brief silence, he turns back to me again. "Would you at least trust me to get your ship back safely? I know I've not been the nicest person to you in the past. I promise to treat the Celeste right, and get her back safely for you." He seems sincere, and even stranger, I do trust him.

"Thanks, Devon. I appreciate that. I'm sorry I got upset. I still don't trust Lewis, but I do trust you. You know the Celeste is all I have. The real question is, do you trust Lewis with your ship?" I laugh, nudging him with my elbow, and end up pushing him off the seat, and knocking myself off balance as well. We find ourselves on the floor entangled, laughing.

We sober up a bit, realizing the intimate position we find ourselves in. We separate, and stand up. Devon looks serious again. "Will you really be all right here with them at the Compound? You might have to wait for the next transport ship to get back, and we don't really know these people."

"Yes, I'll be fine. I'm actually looking forward to learning more about Dr. Kincaid's Project. I've never really studied Earth history before, and after seeing how interested you are on the topic, I think it's about time I start to learn." He smiles, and I look down, avoiding his gaze. "Besides, I'm not in a hurry to face the commander after this whole satellite fiasco." I turn away hoping he doesn't notice the emotions rippling through me. Barely audible, I add, "And I hope I still have a job."

Devon steps closer to me, his solid presence overwhelming in this small space. "The satellite wasn't your fault, Kaci. I promise I'll talk to my father and explain to him about what happened down here. You won't lose your job. Trust me."

I take a couple of deep breaths and nod. I tell myself that I will not cry. This is the last conversation I thought I would have with Devon, and I don't want to act like a total idiot.

I'm saved from trying to figure out what to say next, by the arrival of one of the guys from the demo team. He pops his head through the hatch. "Devon! Oh hi, Kaci." Guess he wasn't expecting to see me with Devon. "Well, I just want to let you know we have stabilized the nukes and are loading them into our secure bay. Dr. Kincaid's team of medics has also fixed up Alex as well as they can, but he'll need surgery on his leg once we get back to the station. Marsh thinks he needs a skin graft on his head, even though it was barely a scratch. I told him the scar will make him actually look less of a girl. No offense, Kaci."

I smile weakly, and say, "None taken." I have worked with these guys for many years now, I should not be feeling so awkward. What is my problem?

He looks back at Devon. "Well, if both ships are ready to fly, we need to get back up. We don't want to miss the last recycler barge of the day, and I don't want to spend the night in this place." He looks up at the storm clouds uneasily, turns and heads back to his ship, leaving Devon and me alone again.

I look at Devon, and place my hand lightly on his shoulder. "I should go too. I need to grab some gear and extra clothes out of my ship. You guys make sure to take good care of my ship." I head toward the door, starting to feel nauseous. "Thanks for taking care of the Celeste for me. I'll see you when I get back." I step outside, and concentrate hard on walking without falling over.

CHAPTER 6

Radiation

I grab a bag of extra clothes from the Celeste and climb into the back of the hovercraft, next to Abishai. The techs and medics are up front. I press my forehead to the window. I watch as my ship lifts off without me, my stomach dropping. It's strange having someone else behind her controls, especially that person being Devon Durrant, of all people. It all seems like a dream, Devon being so nice to me. So many years of him picking on me and competing with me, and now it's as if a switch has been flipped and we've become equals. Maybe even friends?

It then hits me that I'm stuck on this planet, among strangers. Strange how life can twist and turn and change so much, all in one day.

Abishai sits quietly next to me. He seems to sense my need for solitude, and doesn't try to engage in conversation. I appreciate that right now, as so many different emotions roll through me. I watch the landscape speed by as the hovercraft heads toward the group of large buildings on the horizon. The barren landscape is dotted with dry scrub brush and a few stunted trees, desperately clinging to life. Skeleton structures of forgotten buildings push up brokenly from the sandy terrain.

This landscape reminds me of my Lunar trips. The quietness and desolation on Earth's moon is strangely similar to this lifeless road to the Compound.

To avoid being overcome by my emotions, I study the buildings looming ahead. Inside a tall fence that seemingly stretches to the horizon, there are several massive buildings and a low, long building. On the other side of the short building are several very tall windowless, rectangular buildings pushing upward toward the cloudy sky. All these buildings are obviously newer and built with materials to last in this harsh land.

I break the silence. "Abishai, what are those different buildings for?"

He turns toward me and smiles. "The large buildings on the left are for research. We live in quarters below them, underground. It is safest for us there. The tall, windowless buildings on the far side house space ships ready to launch for the final time. The long, short building is where my pet project is." I can hear the pride in his voice. "That is where we build and keep all the drones I have designed. They are each programmed with a location around the globe where they will, on our command, fly to and release the Eugenesis Project serums."

"Do you really think the Project will be able to regenerate the Earth?"

"Yes, eventually, if we can get it implemented before we are ordered off-planet. We have had a few setbacks lately, so we're working round the clock to get it done." He looks back outside the window at the buildings.

"I guess I didn't help with your deadline. Sorry about your transmitter and having to rescue us. That took more time away from your project." I'm afraid now of what he must think of me, with this reminder of what I've cost his project.

Abishai turns to me with those gorgeous green eyes and places his hand on mine. He's very warm and his touch sends tingles up my arm. "If you did not crash my transmitter, I would have never have met you. So, I am not sorry. Besides, you can help me, Kaci. I can tell you can be a valuable asset to my team. Well, after we have finished our radiation treatment." He gives my hand a squeeze.

I smile, glad that he isn't upset at me, but I wonder how long he thinks I'll be down here helping his team. "I'll be glad to help for a little while, only if you promise I can get a hot shower and clean clothes after treatment. I feel like I've been rolling around in a recycler all day." Although I'm self conscious of how much of a mess I am right now, I'm glad that there is a possibility that I can help make up for the broken transmitter.

"I think I can arrange something." His laughter rumbles throughout the hovercraft. I enjoy hearing it, and I find myself relaxing.

The hovercraft stops before an enormous gate set into the thick, solid wall. The wall must encircle the whole

Compound. There are armed guards at the gate, and it makes me wonder why they need such security. Supposedly they are the last humans left on Earth. I know from my limited attention span in history class, that this area was ground zero for the bacteria outbreak, so it would seem the last place anyone outside of the Project would want to be.

Puzzlement must show on my face, because Abishai suddenly looks serious. "They built this wall many years ago when civilization first started collapsing. People were starving, dying, angry. The bacteria was developed here, by my grandfather. It was supposed to have saved us from our selfish, wasteful pollution. When they realized that it had mutated, and that it could not be stopped, the people turned their anger on them. We had many break-ins and bombings here. My father has been trying to reverse the mutation ever since. I grew up here, inside these walls. It is self-contained, and we rarely ever venture out. It is dangerous on the other side of the wall, since there are still small groups of people hiding out in the desert areas. They refuse to leave Earth, and they keep attempting to sabotage the Project. They think that left alone, the Earth will heal itself. But they are wrong. The bacteria will not allow that to happen. There are security forces out there still trying to find these people, so they can be taken up to the habitat ships before we release the Project."

I sit quietly, contemplating all the loss. Even in the vast openness of space, there is still a sense of hope, of moving forward. New planets, new discoveries to search for. But down here, even on solid ground, surrounded by these buildings, it feels empty, bare, and lonely.

We arrive at the first large building. It seems to be made completely out of some sort of thick metal, basically a big box without windows. We drive through a large door in the front. It leads down a tunnel, lit only by a few intermittent lights mounted into the walls. In the weak light I can make out row after row of hovercraft-size doors on either side of this main tunnel. After a few turns we stop before a large door with a big red cross on it that says Medical.

Abishai and I get out of the hovercraft. I notice two armed personnel in uniforms have joined us. I nod in their direction, "Abishai, are we in danger down here? On this side of the wall?"

He looks back at them, then looks down at his feet. "We have not had visitors down here in a very long time, so I suppose my father is just being cautious." Abishai looks back up at me. "My father tends to be a little paranoid. Now that we're nearing the end of the Project, he is more tense than usual. I never know what he is going to do next. I am sorry."

I turn and smile sweetly at the two guards. "I can understand that. I'll try not to cause too much trouble." One of the guards scowls at me, so I turn back to Abishai.

He smiles at me and turns back toward the door. He loses his balance and stumbles against the door jam.

"Abishai," I exclaim and grab his arm to steady him.

He puts his arm around me, gratefully. "Thank you, Kaci. Guess we should get going." We walk through the doors, and a medic team is waiting for us. They notice Abishai's arm around me and give us a few dirty looks. Abishai releases me, and we follow the medics. They take us down a few hallways, all of them white and empty, which feel like a maze. I am totally turned around. I usually have an excellent sense of direction, but apparently only in open space with stars to guide me by. The longer we walk, the more claustrophobic I get. I can feel my anxiety level rising, along with more of the dizziness and nausea from the radiation. If we don't get to an open space soon, I feel like I will explode.

Abishai grabs hold of my hand and gently squeezes. Surprised by the sudden touch, I almost run into the medic in front of me, who has stopped at another doorway. Abishai drops my hand quickly. "Sorry Kaci, I did not mean to surprise you. You looked like you were starting to panic. Is your sickness getting worse?"

I look down at my hands, which are shaking now. Great. "Well, that does seem to be getting worse too. But, it's just that I'm used to either being in open space, or at least in habitats with windows. These windowless hallways that go on forever, they kind of creep me out." Ugh. Could I sound more pathetic?

"I understand, Kaci." He steps closer to me and takes my hand again. His warm smile and touch have a calming effect on me. "I kind of feel the same way when I go outside into the open. I have spent my whole life in these buildings, so for me the walls are a comfort. Just the short trip out to your ship made me a nervous wreck." He smiles, finding humor at our similar situations.

"Other than your bad hovercraft driving, you certainly didn't seem to be panicking. It didn't seem like you had any trouble out there at all. You took control of getting the satellite stable, and you haven't seemed nervous at all whenever I've been with you." I want to take my hand back and turn away so he can't see the rising blush in my cheeks, but I stay put.

"That is only because it was something new and exciting for me. I have not had anyone else my age to talk to. Only the scientists here at the facilities and the occasional supply ship. And you, Kaci, seem to have a way of making me feel comfortable. I feel calm and peaceful near you." It's his turn to blush. Good. I didn't want to be the only one doing that today.

We look away from each other and realize the medic is waiting for us. We follow him into a room that has two beds along one wall. Suspended above each one, are monitors, tubes, and blinking lights. Off to the right is another door set next to a large viewing window. A radiation chamber. It's similar to the ones we have on the station. A shiver runs down my spine, and I feel panic setting in again as remember the claustrophobia of being in a radiation chamber. I was only twelve at the time, but I was working with a team on a ship whose radiation shielding failed. If I thought the hallways here were claustrophobic, radiation chambers are much, much worse for me. Abishai squeezes my hand again, and I try to pull myself out of the panic.

The medic gestures us to the beds. "Please lay down so we can assess your conditions." Cold, clinical, and to the point.

Abishai and I climb onto the beds as a whole team of medics swarm around us. After being poked and prodded, and having our blood drawn, they allow us to clean up. We take sani-showers that have a strong chemical smell. Despite the strong odor, I enjoy the warm water and being able to clean all the dirt and sweat off. They give us simple one piece jumpsuits to wear. Tacky, but at least I feel clean now. We enter the radiation chamber, which is about half the size of the satellite we were just in early today. There is a bench along one side of the chamber, opposite the window. Great. Here we go, more enclosed spaces.

Abishai and I sit down on the bench. I put my head between my knees and take deep breaths. I know we'll have to be in here for a few hours at least, and the enclosed space is already getting to me. I can hear the clicks and beeps as the machine starts up. I concentrate on my breathing.

Abishai leans over and rubs my back. Pretty soon my panic attack has eased up, as I try to concentrate on the warmth of his hand.

I sit up and find Abishai smiling at me. "Feel better?"

"Yes, thank you. I feel so stupid. I've lived my whole life in enclosed spaces. Not sure what my problem is right now." I pull my knees up on the bench and wrap my arms around them. I rest my forehead on my knees.

"Everyone comes across something at one time or another that they are afraid of. You just need to focus on something else to keep your mind off of it, a distraction." A distraction, yes, this boy is definitely a distraction for me.

Soon I feel the panic attack easing up, so I turn and face Abishai. "So tell me, what it was like growing up here, in the Compound. Are there any others our age here? Any brothers or sisters?"

He shakes his head. We look up through the glass as one of the med techs walks by.

I continue. "Okay, so I met your father, but what does your mom do? Is she a scientist too?" I feel him stiffen next to me, and I look over at him. His face is expressionless, like stone. Crap. "I'm sorry Abishai, I talk too much. I'm so sorry if I offended you, or got too personal. You don't have to answer me. I always tend to say the wrong things."

I put some distance between us on the bench and stare out the window of the radiation chamber. The techs are on the other side of the room now, monitoring screens and chatting amongst each other. I guess they figure I can't do too much harm to Abishai in this small space. Boy, are they wrong.

I hear Abishai stir beside me, and I find myself suddenly engulfed in his strong arms. He whispers into my ear as he hugs me tight. "No, Kaci. You did nothing wrong. Nothing." His warm breath on my neck sends shivers down my spine. Then just as suddenly, he releases me and sits down on the floor in front of me with his head in his hands. "I should not have touched you without asking. I am sorry."

I'm speechless. What just happened?

CHAPTER 7

Greenhouse

I slip down on the floor, both of us out of view of the techs, and put my back against the opposite wall, so I'm right in front of him.

"Abishai?" I take both of his hands in mine and finally get him to look up at me. His green eyes are moist and a shade darker than usual. The look he gives me makes my insides all warm. "It's okay Abishai. You don't have to apologize for touching me. I'm the one who is sorry, I must've said something that upset you. Can you tell me Abishai? What's wrong?" I pull him closer to me and embrace him tightly. I feel a shudder go through his body, his breathing uneven. After a brief hesitation, he wraps his arms around me and holds on tight.

When his breathing returns to normal, he relaxes his hold and pulls back just enough to look at me. "Kaci, I have never had someone to talk to like this before. I know it is not the best of circumstances." He looks around at the chamber. "But I am really glad you're here with me." He looks away. "So, about your questions. No, there are no others our age here. I have always lived with adult scientists and engineers. The only time I ever saw anyone close to my age was when the barges would drop supplies off to us. Sometimes they had their families with them. There was one pilot that was my age, but Father would not let me go speak to her. I was amazed someone my age could fly space ships, and I really wanted someone my age to talk with. You actually remind me a lot of her." His eyes are unfocused, and he seems more relaxed now. For once, I stay quiet. I enjoy the feel of being in his arms, his warm body pressed to mine. "I do not have any brothers or sisters. My mom died when I was young. It is just my father and me, and he is not around much. He is always working on the Project, so I was mostly left alone."

"I'm so sorry Abishai, about your mom and your father not being around much either. I lost my father when I was a baby, so it has just been my mom and me. She works a lot, so I was pretty much on my own also." I pull him closer and bury my head into his neck. Beneath the chemical smell, he has a scent of citrus and cloves. I close my eyes and breathe it in, allowing a few tears to escape.

After a few minutes, he leans back and gently pulls my chin up and wipes away my tears.

He looks at me, a small smile playing on his lips. "It hasn't been all that bad, really. I have been taught by all these world famous scientists and had free run of the place. I even have my own part of the Project." He brushes his thumb across my cheek, making my body shiver. "And all my hovercraft training was all worth it, when I almost crashed into your ship. It made quite an impression on you." He smiles mischievously at me.

I laugh and think back about how mad I was when I first saw him. And how rude I was. Talk about not having a filter. "Yes, you did make quite an impression."

We are so emotionally exhausted and lightheaded that we both start giggling. The techs look in the window and down at where we are on the floor. Abishai assures them we're fine, and they eventually go back to their monitors. Even with Abishai living here, they don't seem used to having teenagers around much. Their awkward reaction to our giggling makes us laugh even harder. We end up doubled over holding our sides. Once the giggles finally subside, we stay on the floor, side by side talking for hours. I am surprised to find it easy to talk to Abishai.

Too soon our treatment is finished, and we gather ourselves up and head to the other room to be checked again. I feel pretty toasty from the treatment, but happy after spending so much time with Abishai.

The medics declare us healthy, and we climb into another hovercraft, driven by our armed escorts. More maze-like hallways rush by. Abishai finally has them come to a stop in front of a large set of opaque double doors. Overhead is printed "Experimental". As we go through the sealed doors, I notice our two security guys stay just outside the doors. I'm about to ask what's going on, when I'm hit by a wave of warm humidity; a greenhouse. I look around and see a huge room that reaches several stories high. It's filled with live plants; trees, flowers, grass, bushes. There are real birds flying from branch to branch. I hear chirping, whistling, and other noises I can't identify. This is much bigger than the greenhouse on Jupiter Station. We don't have any birds there yet, just insects and small ground animals. I breathe in deeply, taking in all the colors and scents and textures. It takes me back to all those times I hid out in the greenhouse, reading books. If I wasn't flying, I was in the greenhouse reading.

"This is absolutely wonderful, Abishai!" I can't stop smiling. I feel like I'm dreaming.

Abishai pulls me over to a small pond where there are large stones nearby to sit on. Surrounded by the living greenery and the sounds of bubbling water and chirping birds, I feel like one of those princesses out of the fairy tales that my mom used to read to me.

Except that I'm wearing an unflattering jumpsuit, not a beautiful dress. And in this reality the world is dead, people live in crowded habitats in space, and the prince is the mysterious son of a famous, but grouchy, Earth scientist. Reality sucks.

I shake off those depressing thoughts and find that Abishai is smiling at me, amused and patiently waiting for my inner musings to finish. I smile back at him, thankful he can't read my mind. Before I can even think of some excuse why I'm grinning madly, he leans in and kisses me. I return his kiss, enjoying his soft lips and his clove scent.

We pull back and I put my fingers to my lips. He's smiling and his eyes have darkened again to a deep emerald green. My stomach does a flip flop, as I hover just inches from him. I'm afraid of saying anything, knowing I would probably ruin this moment with my babbling.

As I wonder if we could just go back to kissing, I realize that it has become quiet all around us. No birds chirping, or insects making noise. Abishai and I both turn, and a strong arm pulls me up to my feet. A guard is standing over us, one

48

hand still gripping my arm and the other resting on his sidearm. He's not one of the guards that came here with us. He glares down at me, but addresses Abishai, "Sir, you shouldn't be in here with her." I cringe as he turns his steely gaze from me to Abishai.

My eyes flick between the guard and Abishai. Abishai stands up without breaking eye contact with the guard and reaches over to remove the guard's hand from my arm. He then pulls me to him and puts an arm protectively around my waist. He tells the guard, "She is my guest, and you have no right to treat her that way." Abishai then turns me around and ushers us down a path between the trees. Soon we reach another door and exit into a hallway. I relax into his arms, and we keep walking. At the next junction we meet up with our original guards, who continue to follow us without saying a word.

"Does everyone here hate me?" I try to keep the trembling out of my voice, but it's not working. I know I'm an uninvited guest here and, as far I've seen, the only female in this fortress of a laboratory. I've only just met Abishai less than forty-eight hours ago, and here I am trusting him with my life. How on Saturn's Rings did I get myself into such a predicament?

I stop in the middle of the hallway, and Abishai turns to me. "Honestly, some of the people here do still feel that the rest of humanity abandoned the Earth too soon, that they did not care about those of us left down here. They do not hate you personally." He gently pulls me in front of him, without letting go of my waist. "The whole purpose of this Project, to regenerate Earth, obviously is going to attract Earth Purists, as they like to be called. That guard in the greenhouse is one of my father's advisors and an Earth Purist. They just do not like outsiders."

I let that all sink in. Then I ask, "Do you think those groups will cause problems aboard the Migration ships?" That thought worries me. We have lived pretty much in harmony since most of humanity left Earth, and the Migration will take generations to reach New Earth. That leaves lots of time to either fight amongst each other, or work alongside each other.

Abishai sighs. "I'm not sure, Kaci. All they have known down here is sickness and hardship. The Purists see everyone up in the habitat ships as having it easy. It might be hard for some of them to get over that and try to make it work." He kisses my forehead, and we continue to walk down the hallway.

I wish we could just go back to the pond, just the two of us.

CHAPTER 8

Storm

As we keep walking, I have given up trying to figure out where I am. I rely completely on Abishai. Soon we encounter more people, all in white lab coats, all in a hurry. Another guard approaches us, and I squeeze Abishai's hand nervously. I try to look fearless, but laugh silently at myself. With my frizzy curls and ridiculous jumpsuit, I couldn't intimidate a space rat.

This guard doesn't even look at me. He addresses Abishai, "Sir, there is an urgent call for you and Miss Lee. Comm Station 12." He turns quickly and disappears into one of the many identical doors down this long hallway.

Abishai pulls me through one of the doors. There is a large monitor on the wall and a comm console. Abishai enters a code and allows the scanner to read his eye print. Tight security for the last building on Earth.

I'm surprised when the screen comes to life and Devon's face is staring back at me. "Devon. Is everything okay?" I can feel Abishai stepping closer to me.

Devon answers, "Well it's not a pleasure call obviously." He looks between Abishai and me.

I sigh and answer, "What is it, Devon? And by the way, I'm fine. No more radiation sickness. Just so you know." I thought things would be different with Devon now. I was hoping the time we spent at the crash site would at least lead to some sort of friendship, instead of the usual animosity.

His face softens, his blue eyes holding my gaze. "Sorry, Kaci. I am relieved that you're better. Really. I'm glad you're still safe and in one piece as well." He looks at Abishai with a raised eyebrow, "despite the company you have to keep down there." Abishai just holds Devon's stare. I can see Abishai's jaw muscle clenching.

Devon turns away from Abishai and says to me, "I need to talk to you about your ship." He gives me a questioning look. "Do you want to talk about it in private?" He nods toward Abishai.

I smile thinly and mentally roll my eyes. "No, it's fine. You can speak in front of Abishai."

Devon looks doubtful, but continues, "Okay, then. Some of your mom's creditors want the Celeste. They found out about the satellite issue and you landing on Earth. They want me to bring your ship directly to them. They fear your mom won't be able to keep up her loan payments if you lose your job. So they want to take your ship for payment in full." Anger flickers behind his eyes. Is he not happy with being their errand boy, or is he upset on my behalf?

"Oh, no! Devon you can't do that. I didn't know mom was in debt again. The Celeste is all I have. Is the commander really taking my job away? You said you would talk to him." After all that I've been through the last few days, this is more than I can handle. I feel close to tears, and I have to turn my face away.

"Kaci, wait! I made a promise to you that I would keep her safe, and I intend to keep my word." I look back up at the monitor, and his sky blue eyes are sparkling with emotion. "I'm going to leave her here in Earth's orbit docked to the transport ship, the Excelsior V. The captain is a friend of mine. He'll keep her safe until you can get back up here. I need to return to my ship anyway. Lewis, as you know, is useless and I can't trust him with my ship any longer." He smiles at this and shrugs. "I haven't had a chance to talk to my father yet. I'm sure you won't lose your job, these people are just assuming. I told them I would give you their message, just to delay them." His words tug at my heart. Here I've been afraid of him returning back to the old Devon, but he hasn't. He has put his reputation at risk for me.

"Thank you, Devon. I appreciate you helping me out. Again. Now that I feel better, I should be able to get up there soon, then I can straighten it all out."

"Anytime, Kaci." Devon's gaze flicks over to Abishai, who hasn't said a word. "Just get home safely. We have a lot of work still to do before the Migration. I'll find out when the Excelsior V captain can send a jump ship for you."

Before I can reply, emergency lights and a high-pitched alarm starts up. My hands reach automatically for a space helmet that is not there. Its second nature when we hear alarms like this on Jupiter Station to reach for our emergency suits. Alarms usually mean a containment breach.

"Kaci, what is it?" Devon looks worried.

I look nervously at Abishai. He's looking down at a monitor to his side.

"It is just a storm warning. We get them all the time. We will be all right here in this building, but you will not be going anywhere today. We need to go down to the lower levels for safety. This one looks like a pretty big storm."

"Bad enough of a storm that the jump ship can't make it through?"

"Afraid so, Kaci." Abishai hasn't taken his eyes off the monitor to the side that shows the approaching storm.

I turn back to Devon, pretending calmness that honestly I don't feel right now. "It's okay, I'll wait out the storm. Just tell the captain to keep an eye on the conditions down here, and I'll be in touch. Thanks again, Devon. I owe you one."

"I don't like this, Kaci. This whole mission has gone sideways. And I don't like leaving you down there." He looks at Abishai, narrowing his eyes.

"I'll be fine, Devon. Really. See you in a day or two."

Abishai cuts the channel and Devon's face disappears. Static fills the screen, and then it goes black. I'm now cut off again from everyone I know, everything that's familiar. I face losing my ship and my job. All my years of hard work to earn a scout ship, ruined in one day. A really, really, bad day that has changed everything.

I feel like I want to cry and scream at the same time. I feel stuck, trapped in this room. But where can I go? I would get lost in this maze of hallways. I'm shaking, my anger and anxiety spilling over. I just stand there in the middle of the room, unsure of what to do.

Abishai comes up behind me, turns me around and wraps me in a hug. I melt into his embrace and lay my head on his shoulder. In his arms, I feel safe, for the moment.

At the same time my mind is confused. I can tell Devon has feelings for me. He has put his job and reputation in jeopardy to save my ship. I'm clueless about what to do about him.

Abishai leans down to kiss me again, and I decide that the best thing to do right now, is to not think about anything. After a few wonderful minutes, Abishai pulls back and just smiles at me.

"What?" I ask, suddenly self-conscience.

"I just enjoy spending time with you." He takes my hand and hurries me out of the room. "We need to get below before the storm hits."

"I thought we were already underground?"

"We are, but the secure quarters are down a few more levels. We will be safe in my apartment, and I have comm displays so we can watch what is going on outside." We stop before another set of double doors. These don't seem to have any visible handles, or buttons. He places his hand on a square panel to the side, and it reads his palm signature. More security measures. The doors open and we get into a large elevator. "Level H12, Residence," he says into the speaker. The elevator starts silently downward.

I watch as the digital numbers count down the floors we pass. "Do these storms happen often? And will it cause a lot of damage?" Fear and nervousness tend to make me chatty. Abishai just grins back at me. I'm not sure if I'm doing the right thing, here with Abishai. But I don't move when he steps closer to me.

"Sometimes they do some damage up top, but they are more like dust storms now. There is not much moisture left in the atmosphere to turn into a hurricane or lightning storm. The worst damage, unfortunately could happen to my drones. I hope the crew got the cover over them in time." I can see worry behind his eyes and something more. Is he lying about us being safe down here?

I press my palms to his chest. "I can understand your concerns, Abishai, knowing how important this Project is to you." I draw out the words, watching for a reaction. I chew on my lip, a bad habit from being a nervous child growing up. "But there's something else wrong, isn't there, Abishai? It's more than just the storm and the drones?"

He takes a deep breath and looks into my eyes. I see hurt and fear there, and I wonder what changed so fast, what made him suddenly nervous. "I just do not like storms in general. My father gets agitated with each storm. They remind him how little time we have to finish the Project." He looks away. "It is very bad for me when he gets agitated."

The elevator dings as we reach the floor Abishai has brought us to. We don't move. My stomach tightens into a knot. It's not the storm that scares Abishai, it's his father. Dr. Kincaid isn't the most pleasant of people I've ever met, but there must be something darker going on here than I've seen. Even though my mom is a basket case and isn't around much, I've never been afraid of her. I'm filled with a complicated mixture of feelings. On one hand, I'm grateful that Abishai has shared this horrible truth with me. But, on the other hand, my heart breaks for him. I reach up and place my hands on either side of his head, so he can't look away.

"I'm so sorry, Abishai."

He leans his forehead against mine and takes a deep breath.

Before he can say anything, the elevator doors open.

CHAPTER 9

Waiting

We step out of the elevator, and I feel like I've been transported into another reality. Instead of the white, clinical hallway walls like in the rest of the building, these are colorfully painted in bright reds, yellows, and greens, with rich murals of dancers and musicians. The floor is covered with a thick, deep brown carpet. This reality speaks of home and happiness, laughter and warmth. Quite the opposite of the cold, clinical reality we just experienced above.

Abishai leads me to the end of the warm hallway to his apartment. I have to stop every few feet to study the amazing scenes depicted on the walls. They are very detailed and look hand painted. They are amazing. Abishai doesn't say anything, just smiles at me as I take everything in.

His apartment is just as amazing. The main area has an overstuffed couch, a few quilted chairs, and large monitors covering one whole wall. The other walls are covered with handmade artifacts as colorful as the murals. A small eating area with a food synthesizer sits off to the side. The modern synthesizer and wall monitors seem out of place among the rich earth tone decorations. There is also a large bathroom and two bedrooms. Abishai's is decorated in bold blues with books and strange gadgets lining every wall, and it has the scent of citrus and cloves. The other room is more feminine and decorated in bold, bright colors like the entry hallway. "My mom's room," he answers my silent question. "Father has a room up near the lab. He doesn't ever come down here."

I place my hand on his chest. "Abishai what happened to your mom? You told me she died when you were young, but there is so much of her still here in this apartment. She must have been around for a while, in order to create this wonderful place for you." I realize now, that she is still very real to him, which explains the defensive wall he throws up whenever the subject of his mom is mentioned.

He closes his eyes. I'm afraid I've pushed him too far, and he's going to just completely shut me out. Just as I'm about ready to apologize, he gathers me up in his arms and pulls me over to the couch. The couch cushions sink in with our combined weight. "I have a hard time talking about her, and we can never mention her in front of my father." He shifts away from me and focuses on the dark monitors on the wall. "Also, I do not want you to look at me any differently, or hate me after I tell you her story. I do not want to lose you, after I tell you the truth." He looks at me and I can see so much grief in his features.

"Abishai, whatever it is, how can I hate you? Whatever it is, happened when you were very young. And I'm not going anywhere. Besides, I'm stuck here with you, right?" I tease. "But seriously, I can't even imagine anything you would have to say to make me upset with you, or fear you, because of something out of your control that happened years ago. Please just tell me."

He hesitates, fighting an inner struggle. He closes his eyes again. "When I was little, my parents fought all the time. My father has always been entrenched in his work on the Project. My mom was beautiful and full of life. She had these dark chocolate eyes that, when she looked at me, I just knew she loved me completely. She loved bright colors and everything in nature. She was the one who designed the greenhouse upstairs. And she did love me. We would spend hours and hours in the greenhouse together. I loved being with her." He opens his eyes and looks at me. "I could tell even at my young age though, that although she loved me, she was unhappy with my father. She started her own project over in the taller buildings. The star ships. When things got really bad between them, she created this apartment just for the two of us. She really tried to shelter me from all the tension and fighting, but I knew there was something wrong with our family. Then, one day she was just gone. My father told me she decided to go live in space without us, in one of the habitat ships. He told me if anyone asked about her, I was supposed to say she died." He shrugs his shoulders. "So, I learned to hate anyone who lived up in space as much as he did. I blamed them for taking her away from me." He looks away from me and tries to stand up. I lay my hands on his arm and pull him back down next to me. I can understand now why he thought I might hate him. Like the Purist guard we encountered earlier, he had at one time hated people like me, too.

I shake my head. "No Abishai, don't pull away. Tell me the rest of the story. I'm still here. I'm not afraid of you, and I don't hate you. You were just a kid. One who had to pretend his mom was dead, while grieving the fact that she left without you."

His glistening green eyes search mine. He smiles and holds my hands tight as he continues. "For years I believed the story my father told me, that she chose to travel to the stars and leave me here. As I grew older, I realized that Mom would never abandon me. She would not have filled this place with so much color and life and love and then just leave me. I started asking questions. Most of the guards and scientists were loyal to my father and would not tell me anything. Then, one day, I talked to one of the supply ship pilots that regularly delivered here. He remembered my mom, how she was so outgoing and full of life whenever he would bring supplies for her. Except for the last day he saw her, she was too quiet and looked like she had been crying. She had him take her to one of the transport ships heading off Earth." He shakes his head. "I searched through all the travel records I could find, but I never found any record of her."

I wipe away the tears running down his face. "I'm so sorry, Abishai. After all this, how can you still work for him? Stay down here with him?" I'm angry and sad and terrified, all at the same time. What kind of person is Dr. Kincaid, to have driven away the mother of his son like that? What power over her did he have, that she would leave her son like that?

White strobe lights and chirping alarms interrupt my dark thoughts. I groan and roll my eyes, "Now what? What else could go wrong today?" This emergency, whatever it is, has very bad timing.

"It is a severe weather alert." Abishai pushes several buttons on a remote, turning the wall monitors on. The monitor splits into six different views. The top three are camera views mounted outside the building. They show the storm in full force, swirling so deeply that it looks dark as night outside.

The bottom three screens are cameras inside different lab areas. The lower right one shows the building next door, where we see Abishai's drones being pummeled by flying sand. They look like children's toys being tossed in the wind.

Abishai calls the control room. We find out the alarm was triggered because the winds have reached critical velocity; they are starting to tear into the metal building and are causing damage, even with all the safety doors closed.

Abishai disconnects from the control room. He shakes his head sadly. "There is nothing we can do right now. We will just have to wait it out. We will check out the damage in the morning."

Mention of morning reminds me that I haven't eaten anything today. My stomach grumbles its displeasure. Abishai laughs and pulls me off the couch and over to the eating area. He dials in a few dishes his mom had programmed in the food synthesizer. Her recipes are very different from what I'm used to, but their exotic flavors are delicious, and we devour it all. "Thanks Abishai, for sharing your mom's story with me. And her favorite foods."

"It is wonderful to have someone to share it with. Thank you, Kaci, for listening, for being my friend." He leans down and kisses me.

I stifle a yawn, the day catching up with me. "Sorry. It's been a long day."

He smiles. "I understand. You can use my mom's room to sleep in tonight."

"I appreciate the offer, but I don't think I would feel comfortable in your mom's room." I suddenly feel the exhaustion setting in. "I'll just crash on the couch."

He smiles and whispers in my ear, "Good idea. I don't want to let go of you, anyway." Abishai takes me over to the couch, pulls me down so that my head is lying on his chest, and spreads a blanket over us. He mutes the monitors and turns out the lights. I relax into his arms, allowing my exhaustion to finally overcome me.

CHAPTER 10

Dr. Kincaid

Too soon, I feel Abishai gently lifting me aside so he can slip off the couch. "We need to get dressed." He whispers in my ear. "My father is looking for me, so we can go survey the damage. I had your bag brought down from the med bay." He rubs the collar of the jumpsuit I'm still wearing. "So you can shower and change out of this lovely jumpsuit." He smiles a crooked smile, leans over and kisses me gently. I could really get used to this.

We soon have both showered, dressed, and eaten breakfast. We take our time heading upstairs to find Abishai's father. Neither one of us wants this time together to end.

After hearing Abishai's story about his parents, I know I will have to be careful what I say around Dr. Kincaid. Even though he assisted us with the satellite and allowed me to come to the Compound for radiation treatment, I feel anger toward him for the hurt he has caused Abishai. I don't know how Abishai tolerates him. On the elevator Abishai makes me promise not to say anything, so I will do my best to keep my mouth shut. Although that is not a specialty of mine.

This time we go all the way to the top floor. Stepping off the elevator, I see the whole floor is one large open room. Hundreds of monitors and computer consoles are arranged in rows around the room. There are no windows, just wall sized monitors on every wall, all showing different views.

I spot Dr. Kincaid huddled in the middle of the room with a bunch of stressed out looking men and women in white lab coats. All around them, others are frantically typing and pushing buttons. Dr. Kincaid does not look happy. He's gesturing wildly with his hands and arms and yelling at those unfortunate enough to be close enough to him.

I let my hand drop out of Abishai's grip self-consciously, but he grabs it back with a firm squeeze. I look up at him in surprise and see that his face is set with a look of strong determination and a smile for me that makes my heart race. I draw comfort from this gesture. If he isn't afraid of what his father thinks of us, I won't be either.

We make our way to the frenzied circle of scientists. Dr. Kincaid finally takes notice of our presence. Still yelling to the crowd before him, he gestures at Abishai to come over. When he notices me, he stops in mid rage. His eyes narrow as they lock onto Abishai's hand that is holding mine tightly.

I smile inwardly at his response. We step into the circle of nervous scientists who eagerly step back to let us through.

"Son." A stiff nod to Abishai.

"Dr. Kincaid." Abishai mimics back. A family of many words.

Abishai gets straight to the point, "So what is our situation? You look a bit upset."

I have to bite the inside of my cheek to not laugh out loud.

Dr. Kincaid again glances at our clasped hands. "While you were sleeping, we had a category five storm that caused severe damage." No smile, not even a fake one this time. I guess we are beyond pleasantries.

"I am aware. I checked the monitors before we came up here." Abishai squeezes my hand tighter.

When Dr. Kincaid looks at Abishai, there is no fatherly love there. "The winds are still too strong to get outside and survey in person, but our monitors are showing a lot of damage. We're running out of time. We can't afford any more setbacks!" He glares at me. "Everything I have worked for could be lost. Everything our family has worked for." He slams his fist down on the desk next to him. All conversation in the room stops. His voice has an edge of uncontrolled rage, as redness creeps up his neck. He sticks his finger in Abishai's face. "You need to fix this problem. You need to go figure out how to fix the damage to the drones." He turns his attention to me, and his face contorts into an even angrier version of him, if that's possible. I cringe and mentally ready myself for the verbal onslaught. As much gruffness I have seen among the rough space mechanics, Dr. Kincaid is far scarier. I've never met someone who feels, well, evil. My hands start shaking, and I squeeze Abishai's hand tighter. Mentally I can feel myself shutting down, getting ready to run. I'm horrified that Abishai has put up with this on a regular basis.

Abishai pulls me away, then wraps his arm firmly around me. He steers us back toward the elevators. I can hear Dr.

Kincaid yelling again, ordering Abishai to come back. I'm shaking all over now. Abishai doesn't stop until we are in the elevator. Once the doors close, I crumple against the wall. Abishai embraces me, holding me up with his strong body. "Are you all right, Kaci? I am so sorry! When he gets like that, I just usually take it and let him yell. But I could not let him do that to you."

I reach up and run my hands through his tight curly hair, assuring myself he's really here. I tend to check out mentally when overwhelmed. It then usually takes me awhile before I can come back to reality. Abishai has a very grounding affect on me, and I've already stopped shaking. "Thank you for getting me away from there."

"Welcome." He kisses me gently. "I should have done that with him years ago. That was quite satisfying." He wraps both of his arms tightly around me. He has a sparkle in his eye and a huge grin on his handsome face.

"So, what are you going to do to fix the Project?" I kiss him back.

He unwraps from our embrace and grasps my hands. "You mean what are we going to do about it?" He smiles and kisses my forehead, just as the elevator door opens. This new hallway widens out twice the size of the other tunnels and seems to be at ground level. There are small windows high on the walls, allowing the hazy light in.

We walk over to one side of the hallway where there are small electric vehicles parked along the cement walls. Abishai unplugs one and we get in.

"Okay, now what Abishai? Where are we going?"

"First, we are going to take the underground tunnel over to my lab. It is underneath the drones."

I laugh. "Hopefully you can drive this better than the hovercraft." I make a big display of looking frantically for a seat belt.

"Ha-ha. So funny. That was different. Hovercrafts are high off the ground. I think only real pilots should be allowed to drive a vehicle off the ground." He smiles and nudges me with his elbow. "These cars ride on the ground. I think I can get us there in one piece."

I look behind us, startled by a sudden noise. There are two guards getting into another car behind us. "Are they loyal to your father, or you?"

"These two are with me. They have been with me since before my mom disappeared. They do not like what my father is up to, or how he treats me. They will keep us safe and keep my father's people away from us."

"But isn't it his money that pays for them? He could just order them to spy on you, or turn against you in some way. Enough money could corrupt even the most loyal person."

Abishai laughs, a low rumble in his chest. "You have a suspicious mind." He starts up the car. "No, their pay comes out of a trust fund my mom set up for me. I make sure to use her money instead of his for anything that is important to me. That way he has no control over me. It really makes him mad, but he cannot do anything about it. Seven years after she went missing, I was allowed to access the trust fund. Her family was very wealthy, apparently. I do not think they liked him much, even before Mom disappeared."

"Do you ever see any of her family? Do they visit you?"

"No, none of them have ever tried to contact me that I know of."

"Do you think your mom and her family made it safely to one of the habitat ships?"

"I hope so. I have not had any success finding out. Maybe once we get up into one of the habitat ships, I'll be able to find them. First though, we need to get the Project back on track. We need to finish before the last transport ship is scheduled to leave." He flashes that wide smile that makes my heart skip a beat, and we head down the hallway, followed by the two guards.

CHAPTER 11

Space History

The tunnel starts a gradual climb upward. It's obvious when we connect with the other building, as the hallway here is rough cement, instead of the smooth white walls we just left.

On the rough cement walls are hung old pieces of metal of different sizes and shapes. They are fitted together like a colorful puzzle piece mural. Many of them show pictures and logos of old world rockets and early space ship designs.

"Abishai, what is this? It's beautiful." Abishai stops the car so I can get a good look at the walls. In the back of my mind, I have seen these shapes and pictures from somewhere. I unbuckle and get out of the car. I run my hand over one of the thick pieces of metal that has a blue and red design.

"I can see the wheels turning in that pretty head of yours." Abishai gets out of the car and comes to stand next to me. "Think early space race era. When the world was still whole, but made up of many, many fractured governments."

I grin when it finally comes to me. "NASA! This is the NASA symbol! And over there is the logo for the International Space Station!" I spin slowly in a full circle to see all of the hallway. That's why the metal looks so old, these metal art pieces are all part of Earth's past. "You have original pieces of what, space ships? Buildings? Signs? And you welded them all together? This is incredible!"

"Yes. While Father was busy with the Eugenesis Project, Mom was collecting old world space ships, trainers, pods, and miscellaneous parts. She has dozens of warehouses full of ships and parts. We even have a few working rockets and shuttles she had preserved, in such a way that the bacteria couldn't destroy them. Mom always told me there would come a time when we would need this old technology again. Of course I was so little, I had no idea what she was talking about."

Abishai runs his hand over the metal piece nearest him, with a faraway look in his eyes. "When I was old enough, I went through every single warehouse. I used parts to construct this building and my laboratory for the drones. My father was so mad. I showed him the drones really would work, even with old world technology. He had no choice but to let me finish building a whole fleet of them."

"Nice. No wonder he is so upset with you." As smart as Dr. Kincaid is, he couldn't have pulled off this project without his son.

We get back in the car and continue down the hallway. I make Abishai stop a few more times so I can look closer at the different parts of history passing by us. I feel like a kid in a candy store, and I'm sure I'm drooling. Even our Jupiter Station museum doesn't have this much actual hands on space history. Most of the buildings and technology on Earth—that which wasn't destroyed by the bacteria—was recycled to build the habitat ships.

The hallway suddenly opens up inside a gigantic building. Rows and rows of machines bigger than hovercrafts sit upright like miniature rockets waiting to launch. It's amazing how many there are. The building has a high enough ceiling to accommodate them and stretches on for what seems like miles.

As I look toward the far side of the building, I can already see some of the damage from the storm.

"These are your drones? You built these from recycled parts?"

Abishai frowns. He sees the damage at the far end, too.

"Yes. It has taken many years to build this many though."

"They are amazing. And you can control all of these remotely?" I'm in space ship heaven.

Abishai just nods. His expression is intense, and he is focused on the broken drones ahead.

We continue down the outside aisle of drones toward the damaged area. Abishai's hands are clenched tight on the steering wheel. As we get closer it looks like there are hundreds of rows of drones that have been pummeled by the storm. The roof in this part of the building looks like it was peeled back like a tin can lid. Outside the gaping hole, we can see that the storm has subsided, but the skies are still gray and threatening. The wind, although not category 5 anymore, is still rattling through the building. The drones are scattered as if a giant child has come through here and just started swatting them around. Some are stacked on top of each other, some are missing pieces, some are totally crushed flat. My heart sinks. Abishai has worked so hard on these, and this Project is so important. I can see why Dr. Kincaid is so mad. Even if Dr. Kincaid finishes his part, if we don't have the drones, there is no way to distribute the Project serums all over the Earth.

Abishai stops and gets out of the car. He walks over to a console on the wall and starts typing. His shoulders slump and he rubs his eyes. He looks so exhausted and defeated. I walk over to him and put my arms around him. "I'm so sorry, Abishai." He responds by hugging me tightly to him. Pulling away slightly, he touches his forehead to mine. He gazes into my eyes and I can see that the fight has gone out of him.

"How bad is it, Abishai?"

Abishai pulls away and looks out over the drones. "Not only are most of my drones destroyed, but the drop plane was destroyed as well. It is too big for this warehouse, so I kept it out behind this building. It would take months to fix." He turns away from the carnage of metal. "The United Council has ordered us to evacuate Earth in five days, with or without the Eugenesis Project finished. So, we have failed."

Before I can say anything, I am surprised by red lights flashing all around us. They are on all the perimeter walls, at every console and near each doorway. Then they stop.

"Now what, Abishai?"

He groans and gives me a lopsided smile. "Great. That means my father is on his way here. I installed the warning system when I first started working with space technology, so he could not sneak up on me." He shakes his head. "But now I deserve his rage. I have let all of humanity down. The Project is ruined." Abishai is near tears.

I take both of his hands in mine and say, "Abishai do NOT give up yet. There are always other options. All we need to do is get the drones at certain locations right? Some of these drones look like they could be easily repaired. Can you still pull off the Project with say, three quarters of your fleet of drones?"

Abishai looks across the sea of drones. "I do not know. If we could fix enough of them, I could rewrite their programs to increase their effective spread area. The biggest problem is getting them to the appropriate locations. The ones for this continent can fly under their own power, but the ones that were meant for all the other continents were supposed to be dropped by the now-destroyed plane." I can hear frustration and resignation in his voice, and my heart breaks for him.

At that moment Dr. Kincaid and his crowd of sycophants come through the doors nearest us and rushes over. I back up into Abishai, like a human shield. He rescued me from Dr. Kincaid's tirade earlier; now it's my turn.

Dr. Kincaid starts yelling at Abishai and gesturing wildly at the drones that lay around us. I feel Abishai shrinking back farther behind me.

I step forward. "Stop, Dr. Kincaid! Abishai is not to blame for the storm damage. He has worked hard on these drones and feels sick about the damage. But yelling at him is not going to fix this." As I gesture around at all the broken drones, I wish I had a holo vid camera just then. The look on Dr. Kincaid's face at someone actually standing up to him, makes for a priceless moment. But, unfortunately, the moment doesn't last long. He starts in again, yelling even louder this time.

He rants on about his status with the United Council and how this failure will ruin his career and his future. How Abishai has ruined all the work their family has put into the

Eugenesis Project and now humanity will never be able to set foot back on Earth. His words both enrage me and give me an idea.

I take Abishai's hand firmly and turn to face Dr. Kincaid. I hold up my free hand to stop his tirade.

"I have an idea that will save your precious Project. You have never appreciated Abishai's genius, but we will show you how small-minded you've been. Go back to your stupid lab and get your part of the Project finished and ready to go. In forty-eight hours we will be ready to deliver the serum. I promise you that." I push through the gathered crowd still grasping Abishai's hand firmly. I hope I'm going the right direction. I see out of the corner of my eyes Abishai's guards taking up position behind us, blocking Dr. Kincaid or the others from following.

As we walk, Abishai leans his head close to me and whispers, "Are you crazy, Kaci? Talking to him like that? And what idea are you talking about?"

"Well, first of all you need to take me to your main control room. The one that controls the shuttles and the other old space flight vehicles you told me your mother recycled. Then I'll explain my idea." I really sound much more confident that I feel right now, as I will my legs not to buckle.

Abishai turns us in a different direction, and we are silent as he leads me down more hallways and up elevators. I decide I'm really getting tired of elevators. Finally, we enter a large room with rows of consoles that are tiered with a large monitor taking up the front wall. I smile, recognizing this room. This setup is designed as a replica of a NASA flight control room. Boy, my flight instructors back home would give up a week's dessert rations to see this.

Despite the severity of the situation, I'm soon grinning like an idiot. "You even managed to replicate this?" I look over at Abishai, and he's grinning back at me.

"Actually, it is the real thing. Mom had it dismantled and re-built here." He looks proud.

I give him a big hug and then head over to the main console, shaking my head. "Amazing! I really wish I could have met your mom."

Abishai has followed me and takes my hand. I like that he always has to hold my hand, or wrap his arms around me. "Kaci. Now you need to tell me what your big idea is. I cannot believe you said those things to my father. Thank you. Even if we do not fix this mess, I really appreciate what you did back there."

"You're welcome, Abishai. Now, we're even." I step on tiptoes to give him a quick kiss. "His tirade triggered a story I learned from one of my history lessons. And from what you told me about all the equipment your mom salvaged, I think we can do it. You said she had one of the old shuttles that she kept in working order, right? Just in case it was ever needed?"

A grin slowly makes its way across his face. "Yes, the Endeavour. Right now she is stored underground, but she is on a launch pad that rises up to ground level to lift off. She should be just fine. This control room was built to launch her pretty much automatically. We should be able to do it. But how is a shuttle going to help us?"

I sit down in the command chair, fingering the controls. "We are going to use her to take your drones up to space. We will need to work around the clock to fix as many as we can and then load the serums aboard them."

Abishai looks serious now. "I still do not understand. We cannot take all of them up in the shuttle bay, even if she works. It is too small to hold them all. Only a few would fit. And then what? The shuttle was not meant to fly within the atmosphere for extended periods of time. She takes a lot of old fossil fuel. And who is going to fly her?"

I look him right in the eye. "I'm going to fly her." I don't look away. He needs to know how serious I am, even if I'm not completely sure myself that this will work. "Well, we're going to fly her. Only up to space. We're going to use her to take us up to my ship. The Celeste is still docked with the Excelsior V, where Devon left her. We can dock the shuttle to the Celeste, transfer the drones, then we can use my ship to drop the drones at your specific locations. We can then bring the Celeste back down here and load up more drones. Devon had them fuel my ship, so we should have plenty of fuel for the trips we'll need. We just need the Endeavour to get me up to my ship."

I see Abishai wince when I mentioned Devon, but he doesn't say anything about that. Instead, he stays on topic. "Do you think you really can fly this shuttle? I know you're a good pilot, but I imagine the shuttle is quite different. Older technology than you're used to, as well."

I laugh. Of all the things that could complicate my plan, this is not my worry. "Yes, I can. If there is one thing I'm confident about, is my flying ability."

I stand up and move closer to Abishai. "Now, the question is, do you trust me?"

Without hesitation he answers. "Yes, Kaci. I do trust you." He wraps his arms around my waist. "I think you and my mom would have gotten along well." He kisses me firmly on the mouth. I then lay my head against his chest to feel his heart beating. I wonder as I listen to its steady rhythm if my crazy, risky idea will actually work and if we will survive it.

I startle as someone clears their throat behind us. I let go of Abishai and turn around to see one of Abishai's guards standing there. "Sir, if we're going to get this shuttle flight ready, we better get going." He smiles at Abishai, but does not acknowledge me.

"Thank you. I appreciate your support, Caleb. How many others do we have?"

"There are eighteen of us. All loyal, trustworthy." He then looks at me. "Miss Kaci, do you think this is really going to work?" I see fear in his eyes, tinged with something else. Distrust? Maybe he's just being protective of Abishai.

I try to ignore my doubts. If Abishai trusts him, then I needed to as well. "Yes. As long as your crew can patch together as many drones as you can, I can fly them to the locations. Do you know if you have any old defunct missiles hidden somewhere as well?" I grin. Since I crashed on this planet, I finally feel in control and in my element.

He looks at me, confused. "Well, yes, along with the shuttle Madam Kincaid restored. There are about fifty of them. They were unarmed before she put them in storage. Any kind of explosives, nuclear or otherwise were taken out, of course."

"Good, I don't want them for their explosives anyway. We will use them in place of some of the damaged drones. A waste of good recyclable metal, I know, but at least they offer us more ways to deliver the Project serum. Between the missiles and the undamaged drones, I think this can work."

I turn to Abishai. "What do you think? Am I crazy? Do you think it will work?" I find myself nervously waiting for his answer, even though I know deep down I can make this work. I have never trusted anyone like I do Abishai, and I have never, ever cared what others thought about me, or my ideas.

Abishai grabs me up in a hug and pins me to him. Into my ear he says, "No, I do not think you're crazy Kaci!" He laughs and pulls away slightly. I see that his eyes are sparkling again. "I do trust you, and I feel somehow my mom knew we would need all this and set us up to succeed. I do not know how she could have seen this coming, but I am grateful she had such foresight. Now let us go look at that shuttle!"

CHAPTER 12

Shuttle Endeavour

Abishai takes me down more elevators and white hallways. Once again I'm thankful he knows this place so well. Being enclosed in these windowless hallways and rooms makes me anxious to be out in space again with just my ship and the stars.

We come up to a set of double doors that are locked tight. There is a hand scanner, but also a retinal scanner and a keypad to type in some passwords. I look at Abishai in confusion.

He shrugs and answers my unspoken question. "Mom wanted to make sure my father never got in here. She kept her special projects here. I guess they did not trust each other, even back then. She always kept me with her and never let him take me on his trips to the Council."

"How long has he been on the United Council? I didn't know he was one of the representatives."

"He has been part of the Council ever since he started the Project. In the beginning, after the bacteria, there was the Earth Council of United Governments, and the Space Council. He was on the Earth Council, very much in control because of the Project. When the Councils combined, he remained a voting member, and they still gave him funding and support for continuing the Project."

Abishai punches in the last number on the keypad, and the doors open. I am just getting used to all these buildings and the large amount of space in them, but this one is exceptionally large. And completely empty. I panic, thinking Dr. Kincaid found a way to sabotage the shuttle project. "Where is it? Did he get to it somehow?"

"No, she's here. She lies underneath us. This floor tilts up when she ascends and acts as a blast shield."

I look carefully and see that large square doors with hinges are set into the floor. "Nice!"

Abishai takes me over to the side wall, where we enter a small, open elevator, just big enough for two of us. Caleb and the other guard head over to a console nearby. As Abishai and I descend lower, I can see the tip of the shuttle, and then the main part of the shuttle comes into view. "She's amazing! I've only seen these in holo vids. She's been kept in great condition!"

At the bottom, a team is already getting her ready. I'm relieved that they seem to know what to do. I'm pretty sure I can fly this thing, but I've never worked on engines quite like these. I say a silent thanks to Abishai's mom. She was a smart and resourceful woman.

Abishai takes a call on the hand comm he is carrying. Sounds like other team members are already sorting through the drone mess back at the hanger.

When Abishai is finished, I turn to him and nod my head toward the shuttle. "Ready?"

But instead of heading to the shuttle, he leads us to a side room where there is a simulator trainer.

"Kaci, I do not know how much help I am going to be flying this thing. You saw how much trouble I had with the hovercraft."

I sit down at the simulator. Without looking up from the machine before me, I answer, "That's all right Abishai, these things pretty much just go one direction: up. The tricky part will be docking with my ship. That is when I'll just need you to help monitor the proximity readouts for me. My ship has a tractor beam to guide us in. Don't worry. I'm used to difficult docking procedures." I grin and give him a playful shove. He grabs me in a bear hug, gives me a quick kiss, and then we separate to get to work.

A few hours later, I'm pretty sure I have a good grasp on flying the shuttle. She is an amazing feat of technology. So many parts put together to make a whole ship. Now, with our technology, we've been able to simplify our designs since this era of shuttle craft.

Abishai has been keeping tabs on the rest of his team, and they are making good progress. Looks like they were able to salvage about two-thirds of the drones, so we won't need as many missiles, thankfully. The missiles are taking the team more time to retrofit for what we need them to do. We still haven't heard from Dr. Kincaid, so we're assuming he will have his part of the Project ready. In a moment of panic, it crosses my mind that maybe Dr. Kincaid is a fake, and he really hasn't discovered a way to regenerate the Earth. I look at Abishai and how hard he's working on all of this, and I push that thought aside. I need to keep moving forward, and humanity needs this Project.

Just then, one of Abishai's staff calls us to come up to the main control room.

As we walk into the control room, he motions us over. Caleb is on the other side of the room and turns when we walk in. The first guard addresses Abishai. "I was looking through the file system to make sure we had found the locations of all the missiles your mom tucked away. I found something strange, though. Your father has a new project active down in one of the other old shuttle bays on his side of the complex. I can't tell what type it is, but it looks like a very, very large ship. A space-ready ship, possibly a transport ship. Did you know he was building something this big? And what is worse, it looks like it is armed. With active nuclear weapons."

The look on Abishai's face goes quickly from confusion to anger.

I speak up quickly. "I don't understand. Abishai, what does this mean?" I look between him and the guard. I feel like I'm missing an important piece of this puzzle.

Abishai slumps down in a chair. He rubs his hands through his hair. Despite the seriousness of the situation, I can't help but smile at this unconscious gesture of his. I feel like I have known this handsome boy in front of me for a long time, even though it has only been several days since we first met.

Finally, Abishai answers. "I have suspected something like this from him for a while. I had hoped my suspicions were wrong. I thought he was too busy with the Eugenesis

Project to concentrate on anything else."

He looks up at me. "You know how I've told you how connected with Earth politics he has been? Even while we were working on the Project, he would leave to go to Earth Council meetings, even after the United Council was started. They kept a small, secret Earth Council. He would never tell me what they discussed. He has kept me effectively cut off from all outside communications. No wonder he was so upset when you landed so close to here." He stands up and looks at the data the guard has in front of him. "I think he's terrified you will give me access to off world communications, or that we will find out things he does not want me to know. We need to act quickly to finish the Project, before he goes through with whatever other plan he is working on."

I look nervously over at Caleb, who is still standing across the room, watching us.

"Abishai, do you think he would block us from finishing the Project?"

Abishai shakes his head. "I do not know. I do not really think so, but I also never thought he would resort to using weapons for any reason."

"So, what do you think his plans are with those? After dealing with the nukes in the satellite, I don't want to leave any other weapons like that down here."

"Kaci, I don't think he plans on keeping them down here. Our first phase of the Eugenesis Project will destroy anything on Earth. Those weapons would only interfere or get destroyed. He can't keep them here. That is why he worked with you and the others to get that satellite off Earth, because we do not know what the nuclear material would do to our serums."

Abishai stands up and paces in front of me. "I think he is going to take them out to Jupiter Station. He can use the threat of the nuclear weapons and his position as the creator of the Eugenesis Project and 'savior' of the future Earth, to put himself as head of the United Council. He could then control what is left of humanity and the whole Migration." He stops and looks at me with fear in his eyes.

A cold shiver chases up my spine. I know Dr. Kincaid isn't a very nice person, but this takes his anger issues to a whole other level. "I don't know Abishai. Do you think he's really capable of all that? Does he really want power that badly? He has quite a bit of power already." Can one person be that conniving?

Abishai shakes his head. "There is a peaceful balance of leadership now, with the United Council. People have survived decades of death all around them, no one up there thinks about war anymore. He knows this. He has worked his whole life on this project, and he feels like he deserves the power."

My voice sounds desperate, as if I am willing this whole situation to not be true. "But, he would be endangering his own people. Well, what is left of humanity. We've already lost billions of lives since the original bacteria hit. Would he truly risk what's left of us?"

"I do not think he cares. You do not know him like I do. He is very capable of this. I think this is why my mom left. I think she probably meant to take me with her, but he probably found out her plans and made sure she could not. It all makes sense." His tone has turned bitter, and he suddenly stops pacing and stares at the floor. "Okay. We need to get going on this."

Abishai looks over at Caleb, who has been listening to our conversation. "Caleb, you make sure the drone crews finish up quickly. We have another job for them when they are done. I will let my father know when we're ready for the serums. Kaci, we need to get in touch with the transport ship above."

Caleb gives us a stiff nod and heads down the elevator. Abishai walks out of the control room.

I follow after Abishai, as the others around me hurry to their assigned tasks. Was it just last week that I was happy to be flying around recycling space junk and avoiding the Misfits? Now look at what I've gotten myself into.

We reach a comm room and sit down at the large console. Abishai looks at me. "Okay, Kaci, let us try the Excelsior V." I give him the codes and we dial them. No answer. Abishai tries again. Nothing.

"Let me try something, Abishai." I type in a special distress code after the receiver code.

The comm crackles to life. "Kaci! Kaci, is that you!" It's Devon, although I can barely hear him. What the heck is he doing on the transport ship? He told us he was heading home.

"Devon? Yes, it's Kaci. Abishai and I need to talk to the Excelsior's captain, but why are you still there, and what are you doing answering their comms?" I feel sick to my stomach. Something is very wrong.

"We have a bit of a situation up here, Kaci. The United Council tried to force us to leave orbit without retrieving you. They heard you had instigated a rebellion down at the Compound, and that they were going to deal with you themselves. Did you really start a rebellion?"

I groan. "No, of course not. Great. Dr. Kincaid strikes again. So, if they ordered you all back to Jupiter Station, how come you're still on the transport ship?"

"I promised you to keep the Celeste safe, right? I'm not going to leave you down there, no matter what kind of trouble you've caused. I made the rest of the crew leave, but the Misfits and I stayed to run the Excelsior. What exactly did you do down there, Kaci?"

I roll my eyes. Where do I start? "It's such a long story, Devon. I didn't really do anything. I guess Dr. Kincaid has been busy contacting people up there, making trouble for me. I seem to be a threat to his plan, whatever that is. I appreciate that you stayed for me. We really need my ship. Our first problem down here is that the storm destroyed a lot of the Project drones. So, we came up with a plan to use my ship to spread the drones across the globe. The second problem, which makes much more sense now, is that Dr. Kincaid has built another ship. An armed transport ship. We think he might be preparing to take over the United Council, somehow."

Silence. Abishai and I look at each other. Will Devon believe us? Will he help us? He could easily take off with my ship to avoid trouble.

"Wow, Kaci. When you get yourself in trouble, you do it big time. So, what can we do to help?"

I let out the breath I was holding and smile at Abishai. "Thanks, Devon. Abishai and I'll be up there in about two hours. Just make sure not to let Dr. Kincaid, or anyone else get on board that transport ship. We will explain when we get there."

"Seriously, Kaci? How are you getting up here?"

"We're going to fly the shuttle Endeavour up to you, Devon."

"What? You mean one of the old NASA shuttles? Where the heck did you find one? And how do you know it will still fly?"

I laugh. "Yes, Devon. I told you, long story. Just be ready for us. Once we get this thing on the launch pad, Dr. Kincaid will know we're serious. We need him to think everything is going according to his plan. Be careful up there."

"I will, Kaci. You, too. And did you say, 'we'? He's coming with you?" He points straight at Abishai. "Do you really think that is a good idea? He's Dr. Kincaid's son, and he did nearly take out our ships with a hovercraft."

I stifle a laugh, looking over at Abishai. Abishai looks at me with mock horror. At this I give in to a fit of laughter. "Yes, Devon, he will be great as my navigator. He has a solid team down here that will take care of everything else."

We log off the comm and go to find Caleb.

We find him hunched over a computer terminal. He seems to have taken on more of a leadership role with this crazy project. Abishai walks over to him. "We reached the ship, Caleb. They had some issues, though. Seems my father's influence is further reaching than we thought. The United Council ordered the last transport ship to leave us and return to Jupiter Station. Kaci's friend stayed against orders, so we need to act quickly. We also need to make sure all of our people make it up to that transport ship."

Caleb clears the screen in front of him and stands up. "Okay, Abishai I'll think of something. Right now, we need to get you two into the shuttle. We heard from your father, and his team is already loading the drones and empty missiles with the serums."

Abishai grabs my hand and we start toward the door. "Great, let's go then." As I walk by Caleb, he has a strange look on his face. His eyes flick from the empty computer screen back to Abishai. "I'll meet you two down there."

CHAPTER 13

First Flight

We jog down the corridor to where we can access the catwalk to the shuttle. A team helps us into the old, bulky space suits and get us settled into the cockpit. I feel that old ache to just get out of here. Get out into space.

Finally, the signal comes that everyone is in place, and we are ready to go. The metal doors overhead groan open, not having been opened in a very long time, and the giant elevator slowly takes us upward. A second set of doors in the warehouse ceiling part, and then we're out in the open. The wind has calmed down some, but it still looks like it might be a bumpy ride. I sure hope this thing still works. Sitting atop hundreds of gallons of flammable fossil fuel makes me extremely nervous. I remind myself that I am a space pilot. I can do this. This is what I've been trained to do.

The countdown begins and soon I feel gravity dragging me down, as the shuttle slowly moves skyward. I turn my head slightly to look at Abishai. Through his helmet I can see that he looks terrified. I was so focused on my own thoughts, I forgot that he's never been in space and doesn't like heights. Crap.

"Abishai, how are you doing?"

He shakes his head. "Not liking this part right now, Kaci. Riding in the hovercraft was bad enough. This is, well, much higher." His beautiful green eyes are dilated in fear.

"Just close your eyes and imagine you're one of those colorful birds that fly around in your mom's greenhouse. Flying comes naturally to them. We are just using a lot of gas to fly with instead of wings. I won't let anything happen to you, Abishai. This is what I'm good at." I give him a big grin before he closes his eyes.

To the team I say, "Almost to second stage. We'll be blowing off the first fuel tank in five." I can't stop smiling, even as I'm worrying about Abishai. This is my element. I love being in space, being in control of a space ship.

I say to Abishai, "There will be a little bit of a bump when the tank goes." He just nods, keeping his eyes squeezed shut.

We hear and feel the separation, and Abishai gasps. "That was a bit of a bump? Goodness Kaci, I do not know how you can stay so calm." He's sweating now and breathing rapidly.

"Abishai, open your eyes. Look at me! We're fine. Just concentrate on my face and my voice. Don't think about anything else. Okay?"

"I am trying, Kaci." He still won't open his eyes.

I continue in a soothing voice. "Now, we're going to do a maneuver where we'll be turning. You'll feel us rolling a bit. This old girl is doing really well. Honestly. Why don't you tell me more about what your mom said about these old space shuttles?" I'm communicating with the ground control through the keyboard comm now, so I don't freak out Abishai any more than I have to. So far, so good.

Abishai's voice is shaky, when he finally answers me. "Mom said that they lost a couple of these shuttles in freak accidents." He pauses. Great, he's scared of flying and she tells him about the bad stuff. "But she did say they learned from accidents and improved the shuttles. The space engineers took that technology even further. She wanted to help them with their research, but Father would not let her. So she started repairing and improving the old technology that she could find on Earth. Even as young as I was, I could tell that she loved what she was doing and that she was very smart. I think Father was jealous of how intelligent she was."

He opens his eyes and tentatively looks out the view window. We're above the atmosphere now. Just barely. The view he sees is up, away from Earth. All we can see are stars and the blackness in between them. Breathtaking.

Abishai is silent, just staring outside.

"What do you think, Abishai?" I whisper. My heart is racing, and I'm nervous all of a sudden. For some reason, it seems important to me right now for Abishai to think this is as wonderful as I do. Abishai has become a part of my life, and space is my first love, my home. Even though Abishai and all the others will be forced to live out here, I want Abishai to see it as wonderful and impressive as I do. So, I hold my breath, waiting.

"Speechless." Not exactly the answer I expected, but at least he doesn't look terrified anymore.

I smile and let out my breath. I tip the shuttle's nose down slightly so that the Earth comes into view.

Abishai's breath catches. "Wow. That is beautiful. It does not even look dead from up here." Childlike awe spreads over his face as he stares at his home.

His reverence for this new view of Earth fascinates me. "Yes, it's quite a beautiful view from up here. In my history texts it shows that when the Earth's oceans and seas were still clean, the Earth looked like a bright blue ball from up here. It was truly beautiful back then. Now it's just dirty brown all over. But, from this far away it's still impressive."

"Yes, it is Kaci. Thank you for showing me this." He's smiling like a little boy, full of wonder at the view before him.

Alarms go off right then, and I turn my focus back to the console.

Abishai's eyes snap back to the consoles in front of us. "What is that, Kaci? What is wrong?"

I smile at him. "It's all right, Abishai. It's just the proximity sensors. We're nearing the transport ship. Devon will help guide us with docking to the Celeste."

Abishai looks around at all the buttons and screens in front of him. "Is there anything I can do to help with this, Kaci?"

"Yes, you can keep an eye on those readings on the console in front of you. They show the stresses on the outer hull. I'm not sure how this old space technology will hold up to the tractor beam. Let me know if it starts going into the red."

I switch over controls to Devon in the transport ship and let out a sigh. Great. I've gone from trusting no one, to having to trust so many people.

I turn off the proximity alarms and concentrate on my ship as we get closer. This shuttle handles well, but I'm ready to be at the controls of my own ship. I can feel the tractor beams catch, and I glance over at Abishai. He's pale, but he's concentrating on the gauges in front of him. "How are the readings, Abishai?" I'm hoping to distract him to set him at ease.

"They are getting close to the red, but holding steady. How much longer?" A weak smile. I hope he'll feel more at ease once we're in my ship. It could be tough trying to place drones over the whole planet and keep him calm at the same time.

"Almost there. Not much longer." And then over the comm I ask, "Devon? How does it look from your end?"

"Good. Almost connected." The ship jars slightly, and Abishai grips the edges of his seat. "There, connected and sealing the docking hatch. How's your passenger? His heart rate looks pretty high." I can hear a smirk in his voice. He's enjoying Abishai's inexperience and fear.

I look over at Abishai. "He's just fine, Devon. First time off Earth, you know. It's a lot to take in. I think he likes it." I lean over as far as the straps will allow me toward Abishai. Face plate to face plate I look into his eyes and smile at him. He looks more relaxed now and winks at me. I breathe a sigh of relief and sit back.

Once we are fully docked with the Celeste, we unbuckle and head toward the hatch. I climb into the Celeste and am filled with an overwhelming sense of peace. After Abishai boards, we seal off the hatch. Even though Abishai was on board my ship on Earth after the crash, it feels unusual to have him here. More personal this time. He catches me about my waist and turns me to him.

He speaks to me in a low voice. "Thank you for talking me through that and not letting Devon know how scared I am." Before I can answer, he kisses me softly.

I lean into him, and our kiss becomes more intense. I pull back to catch my breath and look into his eyes. I can see the desire there, and his breathing is ragged. I place my hands on his chest. "As much as I really, really, really would like to stay right here with you and continue this, I think we should get the drones unloaded."

He touches his forehead to mine. "I know. I just wish the circumstances were different. That we could just be two normal teenagers. Get some dinner, see a holo movie, spend time doing normal things together, whatever that may look like. Not risking our lives, or trying to piece together plans that may, or may not save the future of Earth." He hugs me to him tight, and I relax into him, enjoying the moment.

I disentangle myself from Abishai and softly say, "I agree. This situation does suck. If we are successful, and we live through this," I say with a nervous laugh, my face feeling warm, "then we will have to try the normal dating thing."

He smiles at me, totally enjoying the fact that I am blushing again. He leans into me and says into my ear, "I like that. Yes, a date. Wherever we are, we will try a normal date." We both start laughing at this, knowing that nothing could be normal after all we have gone through.

CHAPTER 14

Drones

Abishai and I meet Devon down in the hold of the Celeste. We have to transfer the drones by hand from the shuttle to my ship. Lewis has come along to help with the transfer.

In between loads, I stop Devon. "Thank you, for unloading the Celeste at the recyclers. Was any of the cargo contaminated by radiation?"

Devon's presence doesn't make me nervous or anxious anymore. I know I can trust him now. He puts down the box he is carrying. "No, you were lucky. I had to take it to the recycler at Lunar Base. They didn't give you as much for it, but that was the only way I could avoid having to go back to Jupiter Station. How on Mars did Dr. Kincaid get so much power and build his own ship with weapons?" He sends a dirty glance over at Abishai.

"We're still trying to figure that one out. I'm hoping once we get this current situation fixed, and the Eugenesis Project is on its way, we can get a meeting with someone on the United Council."

Devon leans against a large crate. "That reminds me, Kaci, you owe me an explanation of what the heck is going on down there."

"Yes, I know. Abishai and I will explain everything, but we need to do it while we transfer the cargo. We're kind of in a time crunch." I start toward the hatch.

Devon throws his hands up in the air and follows after me. "Guess I don't have a choice. Start talking."

While we unload all the drones from the shuttle bay to my cargo hold, Abishai and I tell Lewis and Devon everything we've learned. A couple of times Caleb calls Abishai to give him updates on how things are going planet-side.

We finish unloading and sit on the floor with our backs against the side of the hold, tired and sweaty. Devon passes around some energy bars and bottled water. Abishai is sitting right next to me, our shoulders touching. Devon sits across from us next to Lewis.

Devon takes a long drink of his water and then sits up straight, his muscles in his arms rippling after our workout. He is good looking no matter how dirty or sweaty he gets. I try not to notice. "Maybe we should try to reach the council now, before we finish the Project. Of course, I'm not sure if they'll listen to us, since we are just a bunch of teenagers." He grins. "Of course, some of us are exceptional specimens for our age." He flexes his arm muscles to illustrate his point.

Great. I'm stuck in a small space, surrounded by way too much testosterone. I ignore his flexing. "Well, I don't think the council chose you as a pilot just because of your physical attributes, Devon." I glance at Abishai and see him narrowing his eyes at Devon. I continue, "You and I were top scorers all across the space boards. Leadership, intelligence, strategy, and of course flying. We can do this on our own. By the time any council member actually reached Earth to help us, Dr. Kincaid will have his ship ready and armed."

Devon shrugs. "All right, Kaci, you're right. I just don't like it. I feel like a sitting duck up here, knowing Dr. Kincaid has that much firepower."

"I know, me too. You just concentrate on keeping this transport ship close by. We may need you to take on passengers. Abishai and I will work on disabling those nukes. Abishai's team is already working on a plan. We need to get going now, so we can start the dispersion of the drones. Have Lewis monitor all wavelengths, so we can make sure there are no humans left outside of the Compound when we start dropping these things." I smile, hoping Devon is still going to be on board with this plan. When we say it out loud, it does sound like a crazy plan for a bunch of teenagers.

Devon crushes his water bottle and throws it at me. "Just because I don't like the plan, doesn't mean you have to worry about me not doing my part. I won't fail you, Kaci." He gives me a warm smile that fades as he turns to Abishai. "And you make sure that nothing happens to her. Got it?" He has his tormentor voice back, and I cringe. Abishai doesn't even flinch. I guess after what his father does to him, a little threat from Devon is nothing.

They both stand up, Abishai standing a few inches taller. "I will not let anything happen to Kaci. I care deeply for her, and I will keep her safe. Besides, she has proven that she is more than capable of taking care of herself." Abishai's green eyes are intense as he stares Devon down. His body language is strong and determined. My body warms at his bold words.

They stare at each other for what seems like an eternity. I can't stand it anymore, so I roll my eyes and break the tension. "All right, you two. We have a lot to do, so let's get to work." I smile and wave farewell to Lewis and walk past Devon toward the control room. "Thanks for your help, Devon. See you back up here as soon as we take care of a few things." I grab Abishai's hand and we walk back to the Celeste's control room and get settled into the command chairs. I check the distribution of the weight that we have added to the Celeste. I hear Lewis and Devon sealing the hatch and returning to the transport ship. Abishai is very quiet, while I complete my pre-flight checks.

When he finally speaks, his voice is even more formal sounding than before, if that's possible. "Devon really cares about you, does he not, Kaci?" His face is stony.

I take a deep breath and let it out. "It's complicated with Devon, Abishai. For my whole life he was really mean to me. I grew up without any friends, and I put my whole heart and soul into flying. Then when we landed down on Earth, it was like he changed into this nice person that I wasn't used to. I think we're just good friends now." I swallow hard, realizing that Devon and I really did develop some sort of friendship, in a short span of time. Had it been hours? Days? My sense of time is a blur.

Abishai squirms uncomfortably in his chair. "And what about me? Do you think of me as just a friend too? I realize I have not known you for very long, and my father turning into some stereotypical mad scientist does not help my situation any. But I really do care about you, Kaci. If you think I am in the way at all though, well..."

I interrupt him by unbuckling my seat belt and closing the distance between us to firmly kiss him. I place my arms around his warm shoulders and bury my face in his neck.

"Abishai, what you and I have, is so much more than anything I could've imagined. I feel safe with you, and I care deeply about you as well. More than a friend." He responds by encircling me with his arms and hugging me back.

I pull back to look up into his face. His eyes are moist, and my heart skips a beat. This connection that Abishai and I have forged over the last few roller coaster days feels strong. My mind is overwhelmed with the reality of all this and the fear of screwing it all up. I hold him tight again and wish with all my being that I didn't have to let go.

But, of course, reality has to intrude. The comm crackles to life, and Devon asks us if we're ready to release the docking clamps.

I scramble back into my seat, while both of us grin like little kids caught stealing candy. I strap in and tell Devon that we're ready. I take the controls and move the Celeste away from the transport ship. Just like that, I'm flying again. I love this ship. With Abishai on board, it is perfect. Well, except for the maniac on Earth with a ship full of nukes and the several hundred drones and missiles we have to get into place before the looming deadline.

I shake all negative thoughts out of my head and focus on the task at hand. We head toward the far side of Earth to drop the drones we have onboard.

As we fly across the dead landscape it looks like the drone towers that Abishai's team placed here are still intact. Below us the scene is eerie with partial buildings and structures lying broken and abandoned. Abishai tells me that the most populated areas were hit the hardest. More population meant less food to go around after all the storage supplies were destroyed by the bacteria. The areas that were less populated and relied mostly on farming and fishing, lasted longer. These hard working laborers already lived day to day and never were able to stock up on food. So they didn't have storage to go bad after the bacteria. Then, the desperate city populations fled to the countryside and killed everyone there for their food. Abishai said this happened all over the globe. Survival of the fittest. Another reason those of us living in space couldn't come back. There really was no safe place to come back to. Everything on Earth had changed in a matter of just a few years. I find it very sobering flying over these places where humanity once laughed, loved, lived, danced, and created art and technology. Now they are places of silent death. Even though Abishai was born on Earth, he has always been pretty sheltered at the Compound. He had never seen just how widespread the actual devastation really looks like. We are both humbled by what we're seeing.

We return to the Compound five more times to load up drones and disperse them. Dr. Kincaid has checked in with us a few times. He can't believe we are actually on schedule with the drone placements. A few times I've even detected a hint of gratitude. Maybe. Hard to tell. In my mind I see him as the typical mad scientist, like in the old holo vids; crazy, misguided, intelligent, and dangerous. Even though we're helping him, I still don't trust him.

Caleb's team has been able to hack into the secure system for Dr. Kincaid's armed ship. We are hoping at the right time, we can just disable the nukes, Plan A. Caleb also has a plan B in case that doesn't work. I'm not crazy about plan B, because it puts my ship in danger along with the lives of most of the people left stranded on the ground. So, I'm really hoping his plan A works.

I've had to fly above the permanent cloud cover twice to recharge my solar batteries, but we finally finish. Abishai and

I head down to meet up with his father. Our crew has everything ready. The drones are in place, and the missiles have been dropped to their locations. We have fixed as many of the damaged drone towers as possible, and it seems we have full communication with the drones. Now to see if the Eugenesis Project really works.

CHAPTER 15

Below the Compound

We land the Celeste in the shuttle bay. Abishai and I still aren't sure if Dr. Kincaid suspects that we know about his armed ship. I'm nervous as we head over to find him. We decided to see this Project through completion and then deal with Dr. Kincaid's secret later.

Caleb and a few other guards join Abishai and I as we get into the elevator to Dr. Kincaid's main lab. This is where the countdown for activating the drones will be implemented. We bring with us the portable control box we rigged up to control the missiles that were substituted for the damaged drones. The first serum will destroy any organic or manmade material on the surface of the Earth, including any of the bacteria left. The second serum, which will be detonated from space, will deliver the life-giving serum that will re-build the Earth and its atmosphere. Although I would like to strangle Dr. Kincaid for all he's done to Abishai, I have to admit, this Project is pretty big stuff. If it really works, Dr. Kincaid will have accomplished the impossible. A newborn world. I just wish he was a better person to deserve all the praise that history will give him.

We step out of the elevator and see they have just started evacuating. The scientists around us are frantically packing equipment and documents. There are so many people still here, I wonder if we have enough jump ships to take them up to the transport ship. We have to pretend we don't know about the large ship.

Abishai strides over to his father and confronts him. "Why have you not evacuated your non-essential staff yet? The countdown starts in two hours. This many people will take longer than that to get off Earth. Not to mention all the equipment we still need to pack." I hold my breath. Is Abishai trying to get his father to admit to having the ship? In front of everyone?

Dr. Kincaid keeps eye contact with Abishai. "That is my responsibility, son. You just make sure your drones and old missiles work. I will not have you ruining me, again." His voice is cold and uncaring, as if talking to a stranger.

"My drones will work just fine, Father."

"Good, then hand over the control box and get her out of here." He glares at me and then reaches for the box in Abishai's arms.

Abishai takes a step back from his father.

"I do not think so. My team and I worked hard on this, and we will see it through completion. And she has a name. Kaci just saved your precious Project. Without her idea for using the old missiles and the use of her ship, the drones would not have been placed in time." Abishai hands the control box to one of his staff and comes to stand next to me. "And unlike you, we have a plan for evacuating our people." Several of Dr. Kincaid's scientists nearby us turn their heads quickly toward Abishai, pausing their packing. "We have enough room on Kaci's ship to take all my staff and equipment up to the waiting transport ship. How are you going to get all your people and supplies up in time?" More heads turn our way, waiting for Dr. Kincaid's answer.

Abishai ignores their stares and pushes on. "You know we cannot delay any longer. The Council has already given the order to the transport ship to leave with or without us once the first serum is activated. You know as well as I do that we have to be far enough away from Earth's atmosphere to avoid the serum's deadly affects."

There is nothing but malice in the look Dr. Kincaid gives Abishai. Dr. Kincaid speaks slowly, each word slicing cold through me. "I have a ship ready that is big enough for all my people and equipment." He glares around at his staff, and they scramble back to packing. "I will not leave my research behind."

Abishai pretends to show surprise. "Really? You did not tell me you had a ship."

"I don't have to tell you everything. Now I have to get back to work." He turns around, signaling the end of the conversation.

Abishai grabs my hand and pulls me toward the elevator. One of his guards follows us, while Caleb stays behind.

When we get down to Abishai's apartment, he instructs the guard to load all of his possessions into my cargo hold. I see someone has already packed up his apartment, and the boxes are labeled and waiting.

After making sure this will be taken care of, Abishai takes me over to a smaller elevator at the end of the hallway. We get in and head down farther into the bowels of this cement dungeon.

"Where are we going, Abishai? Shouldn't we be in the control room? You know, making sure your maniac of a father doesn't sabotage anything? Or double cross us somehow? I'm surprised he just let us go, after telling us about his ship."

"That is why Caleb and his team are there, to keep an eye on him. You and I need to take care of one final issue." He smiles slightly, pulls out a key and inserts it into the elevator panel. He pushes a button at the very bottom, and we descend even farther.

Even though he is holding my hand, he suddenly looks miles away. I can tell from the grim set to his chin that whatever we are doing down here, it's not going to be fun.

The elevator opens and we find ourselves in a dark hallway. The only light comes from small emergency lights lining the floor. Abishai leads me confidently down the hallway and then turns left. The walls here are rough concrete, like Abishai's laboratory. It sounds muffled here, silent, except for our own feet on the concrete.

I whisper close to Abishai's ear, "Abishai, where are we going? What is this place?"

He squeezes my hand. In a quiet voice he answers, "This hallway runs underneath the pad where my father's ship is waiting."

I stop suddenly and pull him close, so I can see his face in the low light. "What? What on Venus's spot are we doing here? He's crazy. If he finds us, well I don't even want to think about how angry he'll be."

"Kaci, we have to take care of the nuclear weapons."

"What? I thought that was up to Caleb? He had some sort of plan A and B." I smile weakly. My voice sounds more desperate than I intended. I hate being scared of Dr. Kincaid.

"I think this is something we need to take care of ourselves. Even if Caleb was able to disable them temporarily, they will still be in my father's possession. I cannot allow him to bring those weapons with him. It would only be a matter of time before he found a way to arm them again. He will not stop whatever political game he is planning with the Council."

"Okay, so what are we supposed to do? Walk in there and carry them out? Even if we could somehow get them past whatever guards he has posted, he would find us. Where would we take them?" I look into Abishai's eyes to see just how serious he is about this plan. His eyes are dark, almost black in this dim light. Dang it. He looks determined and deadly serious.

He pulls me close, his forehead touching mine. "Yes, we can do this. It's my turn to have an idea. I have lived in this Compound my whole life. I know every room and corner. As a kid, I could get around without my father spotting me, no matter what building he was in, or how many cameras he installed. There are many hidden areas."

Quietly he opens a small door in the hallway. I didn't see it there before because of the darkness. Peeking in the room, I see it is very small, the size of a janitor's closet. He pulls me in and closes the door behind us.

Abishai reaches up the wall and feels around. I hear metal scraping on the concrete, and then a crack of light comes on from a stick in his hand. "Here take this, and I'll help you up."

I take the glow stick and look up where he's pointing. A vent. Great. We're going to have to crawl around the ventilation system, where there are creepy crawly things. At school I would use the station's vent system to hide from the Misfits. You would think living in a space station there wouldn't be bugs, but no such luck. They apparently followed us from Earth; something about the greenery in the greenhouse needing them. Ugh.

I let Abishai boost me up, and I wait until he's in before I ask, "Okay, smarty, now which direction?"

He nudges me forward. "We need to take the first left and then a right. Once we turn that corner, we will have to be very, very quiet. That spot is closest to the aft hatch of his ship. I studied his ship's specs before we went to see him." In the green glow of the emergency stick, his eyes shine bright, but that's about all I can see of him in this dim light. I, on the other hand, glow bright all over due to my extremely pasty white skin. I probably look like a ghost all lit up. I smile at that image. Maybe I'll scare the bugs off.

We move cautiously until we finally arrive at the vent. We peek out, but don't see any guards or staff. Strange. That makes me nervous. We drop silently down to the ground and keep to the shadows. Closer to the ship, we see why no one is near the back of the ship. On the other side of the bay, there are at least ten large rockets. Rockets similar in design to the one that powered the shuttle we used. Each one is being loaded with crates.

"Abishai, what could be so important that he couldn't load that on his ship? His ship looks like it would hold tons of storage containers." I have my mouth pressed to his ear, so I can whisper as quietly as possible. He shakes his head and moves behind some crates farther along the wall. We inch our way closer and catch a glimpse of what is in one of the crates, before the worker closes it. Gold bars. Ten rockets full of gold. I clamp my hand over my mouth to keep my surprised exclamation from being heard. This is definitely not what I was expecting.

We move quickly back to the big ship. Abishai settles us in a hidden corner. "I think that is father's backup plan. If the nukes do not work, or do not scare the Council, he can buy the power. He has had all these years without anyone around down here, to mine the gold out of the ground. I always wondered why we had so many workers at the Compound."

"We can't take care of the nukes and all those rockets Abishai. We're running out of time."

"I know. Let's just do what we came here for and somehow figure out what to do about those rockets later. It is very odd though. If he has that many rockets filled and going up, where are they going to go? Obviously the gold will not fit on this ship, or he would have just loaded the gold directly on it. And those rockets will not even make it past the moon, loaded down like that. They will need to have a pretty close destination."

A crash from the other side of the room startles us and we both jump. One of the workers has dropped a container of the gold. They are all milling around like ants trying to pick it up. Now is a good time for us to move.

We make it into the hold of the ship. Although it is a huge vessel, it's pretty easy to find the nukes. The amount of electronics needed for them uses a lot of power, so we follow the newly added power cables to a far corner of the cavernous hold. There are only five of them. Strapped in, ready to go.

"I thought there were six of them, Abishai?"

"I thought so too. That is what Caleb said. Anyway, let's take care of these before we look for the last one." He pulls some tools out of his jacket pockets and starts working on the wiring.

I'm glad he knows what he's doing. Just like with the satellite, electronics are not my specialty. I'm good if you give me an engine to strip down and put back together. Engines are simple compared to electrical wiring.

"Kaci, go over to that storage container by the door. There should be a heavy gray box in it. Bring it to me please."

I find the box and find that it is heavy as he described. I'm out of breath by the time I bring it back to him.

I check outside. Looks like the worker ants are just about finished loading the gold into the rockets. Crap. I rush back to Abishai. "We need to hurry. They're almost done. They'll need to start loading this hold soon with all that other stuff they were packing upstairs."

"I know, it is just a little tricky. I am transferring the last uranium cell to this box; it should have enough lead shielding."

"What! You're actually taking out the uranium? I thought you were just disabling the warheads. Cutting wires or something."

"No, this way they will still look active, but they just will not have the nuclear matter to cause an explosion." He grins and closes the box. "There, done."

CHAPTER 16

Traitor

We head for the door, but we see one of the white coats coming this way. We freeze and look around for another exit. Off to the side nearest us is another doorway, so we head that way. We find ourselves in the control room of the ship. We are trapped, with no other way in or out. We crouch behind one of the consoles and listen. The worker is dropping a load of boxes in the hold. He scoots them in place and leaves.

"Abishai, let's go now before any others start coming in." I look over and see he has stood up and is looking at readouts on the console.

He groans out loud. "We have another problem, Kaci."

I lean over the console to see what he's looking at. It shows a ship, a huge habitat ship and not of any design that I have ever seen. It hovers on the night side of Earth, out of range of any space sensors. "What is that?"

"Looks like my father built two secret ships for the migration. This one is my mom's early habitat design. It is big enough for all the people here and all of the gold they are loading up. I imagine he will just send the rockets to that habitat ship and they can transfer the gold. He will have his gold, his people, and the nukes. And two large ships."

I stare in disbelief at the data before me. "Abishai, how did Caleb miss this? He found the transport ship, but missed the huge habitat ship hanging around the Earth?"

"That is a good question. Caleb is my best computer systems analyst. He has worked on the drones with me since the beginning. That ship is hidden on the dark side of Earth, but I do not understand how he could have missed this. We do not have time to figure it out. We need to get out of here. Now."

A familiar voice speaks suddenly behind us, "That would be a great idea, but you're too late."

We turn around. Caleb stands in the doorway flanked by two other guards from Dr. Kincaid's team. They have our exit blocked.

"Caleb? What is going on?" Underneath the surprise, there is deep pain in Abishai.

"You've always been too trusting Abishai. Do you really think you have more to offer me than a man who will someday become ruler of New Earth?" The arrogant tone of his voice makes my skin crawl. Caleb has been Abishai's most trusted staff and friend all these years. I see out of the corner of my eye that even as betrayal rocks Abishai's emotions, he has still managed to push the box full of uranium underneath the console. Caleb doesn't seem to notice.

"So that is his plan? He wants to be leader over New Earth? With all the lies, does Father even have working serums for the Eugenesis Project? Or is that a lie too?" Abishai is shaking with anger.

"Oh yes, the Project is real. The success of the Eugenesis Project will assure him humanity's gratitude. No one else has been able to save Earth. The hope that someday it will be habitable for life, even if it isn't right now, will boost Dr. Kincaid into history as the most important person to the future of the human race. The Council will not be able to say no to anything he wants; and what he wants is to become leader of what is left of humanity."

"If he is so confident that Project will guarantee him success, why use weapons? Why risk more human lives?" Abishai moves back towards me and places his arm protectively around my waist.

Caleb cocks his head to one side and looks at Abishai. "Haven't I always told you always have a contingency plan? In this case those nukes are plan B." He looks over at me. That's not good. "Now, Kaci, I want you to go very slowly over to the comm and dial up your space friend on the transport ship. You will order him to leave orbit and go back to Jupiter Station, like he was supposed to do in the first place. If he doesn't, we will be forced to deploy the nuke we have trained on him."

The sixth nuke. That's why they kept it separate. I wonder if it's on that habitat ship or somewhere down here ready to launch. We need to stall his plan, whatever that is, until we can find that nuke. "What about the people down here, Caleb? The ship Devon is on, is supposed to take all these people to safety." I try to sound brave, but I think it just comes out as terrified. Dang. I'm not very good in tense situations.

"Oh, don't worry about them. If they swear loyalty to Dr. Kincaid, they will have a place on our ship. If not, then I guess they shouldn't have put their faith in a child." He locks eyes with Abishai. I feel Abishai's whole body tense, readying for a fight. The other guards step into the small room, their presence making the very air feel too dense to breath.

I need to distract them. I force my own terror down and ask, "What about my ship, Caleb?" Good. Anger sounds better than terrified. "What will you do with her?"

"Your ship is no concern of mine. Now dial the transport ship, and be very careful what you say. Your lives depend on it." To emphasize this last part, he has the two guards grab Abishai away from me. One punches Abishai hard in the stomach, while the other keeps hold of him so he can't get away. Someone screams, and I realize it is me. Great. Very brave, Kaci. I fight back tears and come around to face Caleb. "Jerk! That wasn't necessary!"

"The comm, Kaci, now!" Caleb's voice is cold as liquid nitrogen.

I dial Devon on the comm. "Kaci? Is that you? I was worried when you didn't check in." The worry in his voice makes me sick to my stomach. Here he is worried about me, when I know that his ship has a nuke aimed at it. I mentally go through all my options. Chances are if we fight him now, Caleb might find the uranium we took out of the nukes. Not to mention, Devon's transport ship has no way of defending itself. Yep. Screwed.

So I lie. "I'm fine, Devon." My voice is a little shaky. I look over at Caleb, scared. I close my eyes and mentally pull myself together. I speak very carefully, trying not to betray my lies and nervousness. "Devon, I need you to break orbit now and head back." I hold my breath. I know he won't just take this kind of crazy order from me. He knows we have almost a hundred people down here.

"Uh, Kaci, I still don't have those passengers I've been waiting for." Good. He's suspicious enough to think someone might be listening.

"Devon, they have..." I hesitate. Will he get the hint enough to not argue with me? "They have another plan to get these people away from Earth." Not quite a lie. "We don't need that transport ship." Big lie. I look over at the countdown timer. "Besides, we only have forty-five minutes left until phase one of the Project starts. You need to get that ship out of range." Please Devon don't argue.

Silence. Then, "All right, Kaci. We will wait for you at Jupiter Station. I'll make sure to say hello to your father for you." The comm goes dead.

I find myself sweating like crazy, as I try hard not to smile. Devon got the hint. He took the risk that anyone listening would not know that my father is dead. I feel relieved that he went along with it. I hate lying to Devon, especially now that we finally have become friends, but right now I don't see any other options.

On the monitor we watch as Devon takes the transport ship out of orbit. I console myself with the thought that at least he's safe now. I look around the room and hope that Abishai and I will be too. I need to come up with another plan, quickly.

Caleb shoves Abishai and me toward the door, with the other guards close behind. I grasp Abishai's hand tightly.

CHAPTER 17

Tears

We are led up the elevator and down hallways that are already becoming familiar to me. I think back over the last few days since I've been down here. I feel much older than my seventeen years with everything that has gone on. Days ago I was an overachieving, lonely teenage space pilot. I thought only of flying, getting good grades and avoiding bullies. I didn't really think about Earth or its problems. As I make my way to Dr. Kincaid's lab, I'm thankful that, even after everything that's happened, I got to know Abishai. Of course, his father might just kill us today. I sure do have bad timing when it comes to love. I start shivering with fear.

Once again we enter the lab. This time, the staff have all the boxes packed and are heading past us, to load them into the ship. Dr. Kincaid is sitting before both Project control computers. The timer countdowns read 30 minutes left.

"Ahh, despite your attempt at sabotage, Abishai, I am still on schedule with my plan." Dr. Kincaid stands and comes over to where the guards have stopped us. I'm trying not to let him see that I'm shaking with fear. Abishai is slumped over, still nursing the pain in his stomach. Dr. Kincaid notices and yells at Caleb. "What happened here? I told you not to harm my son."

Caleb takes a step back. "Sir, we had to make sure she—" He jabs a finger at me. "Obeyed our instructions in getting rid of that transport ship. This was the only way to control her." Caleb doesn't look so smug now.

"Yes, she's been nothing but trouble since she got here." He glares at me. I try killing him with my best death ray stare, but of course it doesn't work. He still stands there breathing, talking. Stupid reality.

Dr. Kincaid motions, and we are surrounded by several more guards. "We must get her away from my son. She has poisoned his mind with her lies."

Despite the pain in his side, Abishai lunges for his father. "No!" The guards stop him before he can reach Dr. Kincaid. "You are the one with the messed up mind, Father. How can you allow all these people to die down here? How can you do this to your own son?"

"Oh, I don't plan on leaving anyone down here, Abishai. Not even her. Your staff will learn in time, as you will, that I am the hero in all this." He gestures broadly to include all the monitors showing differing views of Earth. "I am the one who will be calling the shots up there, because I am the one who is saving Earth. They are going to beg me to lead them in the migration."

Abishai backs away from the guards and leans in next to me. He puts his arm around me and kisses my forehead. This helps ease my shivering.

Dr. Kincaid shoots me a look of disgust and turns back to Caleb. "Have you prepared the ship as instructed?"

"Yes, sir. It's ready. All comms are disabled, and I left only a few fuel cells."

"Excellent. Take her there now. Make sure she leaves."

Abishai stands between me and Caleb, "What? Father what are you doing? She stays with me."

"No, son. That is where you are wrong. I will not have my son consorting with a dirty recycle pilot."

Abishai lets out a harsh laugh. "You do not get it, do you, Father? You cannot keep me here, I'll go with her. I love Kaci!" Abishai turns back to me, and I can see in his eyes that he means what he just said. He places his forehead on mine, his hands on either side of my face and whispers so only I can hear. "I do, Kaci. I love you. I want to be with you always."

Dr. Kincaid yells, red creeping up his neck. "Caleb! Take her away now! Guards hold Abishai until she is gone and then lock him in my ship."

Caleb tears me away from Abishai and starts dragging me away. I fight as hard as I can, but he only gets more guards to help. I yell over the commotion, "Abishai! I love you too! Don't ever forget that!" I feel my heart tightening in my chest. I can hear Abishai yelling my name. I'm crying so hard, that by the time they get me into the elevator and down the many hallways to my ship, I am numb, shut down. Nothing matters at this moment; not without Abishai.

CHAPTER 18

Oxygen

They strap me into my pilot's chair, and Caleb dials in the commands for lift off. I know I should be paying attention to what he is doing, but I don't.

"Pay attention!" yells Caleb.

I ignore him. I just don't care.

"Kaci!" This time he slaps my face.

Okay, now I feel something. Anger.

"What, Caleb? What? What could you possible do to me right now that I would care about?"

He smirks, igniting more anger in the pit of my belly. "Well, let me tell you little girl. Dr. Kincaid may be going easy on Abishai right now, in front of the other staff, but if you cause any problems or jeopardize his rise to power, he will not hesitate to quietly kill Abishai. Do you understand now? You have no comm systems aboard your ship. You only have enough fuel cells to get you close to Lunar Base. Barely. If you say anything about what you have seen down here, I will personally carry out Dr. Kincaid's order against Abishai."

My face must show the terror I feel, because Caleb smiles. "Yes, it looks like you do understand now. As long as you behave, Abishai will stay alive. If you really do love him, you won't let him die." The sarcasm in his voice cuts into me.

I want to throw up. I want to scream. I want to punch Caleb in the face. But all I can do is nod my head.

"Good, now get going, I have to get back to make sure everyone is boarded and ready to go. Only ten minutes until we unleash the first serum. Very soon history will be made, and I will be a big part of it." He laughs and steps out to seal me in.

I mechanically go through the pre-flight checks to prepare to leave Earth. Caleb was telling the truth for once. I have no comm systems and he destroyed more than half of my fuel cells.

I soon lift off, not feeling that usual giddiness when I'm flying. I find myself looking out the view port at the Compound buildings sprawling below me, as the Celeste takes me up. Somewhere down there is Abishai. I know I won't be able to say anything to the Council. I won't be able to warn them, or even to hint to them at what I have seen here. There is no way I can put Abishai at risk. I don't know if I will ever see him again, but at least knowing that he is alive will comfort me.

As I enter the upper atmosphere, the ride gets a little bumpy. The weather is getting worse. This is why it is important that the Project stay on schedule. If they wait too long, the drones won't be able to fly, or disperse the serums.

As I think about the two serums, I realize that it is so much easier to destroy than to build. Like Abishai and me. It took a few days, a small amount of time really, to create a once in a lifetime bond. We went through radiation sickness and treatment together, we spent hours fixing drones and dispersing them. We talked constantly, sharing our fears and failures, and got to know each other. Abishai was able to get through my personal defenses, and I earned his trust as well.

Then, it took Dr. Kincaid only five minutes to take it all away. One command, one moment in time.

I miss Abishai more than I ever thought I would miss anyone or anything. I slump down in my harness and cry until I don't have the energy to cry anymore.

I wake up from dozing and realize that I can't see Earth anymore. The stars sparkling at me through my view window help break me out of my self-pity. I sit up straight and take stock of my situation. Caleb has programmed the Celeste in a trajectory toward the Lunar Base. There should be ships there, or if they have evacuated already, I can land and find a comm to reach Devon. Maybe.

I have about an hour to come up with some kind of story. Why I ordered Devon to leave all those people down there. Why my comm is disabled. Why my fuel cells are damaged. Why Abishai isn't with me. I sigh and wipe my tear stained face. So many secrets. The only silver lining here is that the Eugenesis Project is on track, and I had a small part in that. It will work, I know it will. I would've had a really hard time explaining the demise of the Project as well. So at least I don't have to tell all of humanity that the Earth will be dead forever. At least there is that. The Earth will be reborn someday.

I near Lunar Base and notice a blip on my sensors. Behind the moon hiding on the far side from Earth is a large ship. At first I think it is Dr. Kincaid's habitat ship, but his ship should be on the other side of Earth from here. This one is a bit smaller, a transport ship. Devon! My heart races. It could be Devon, but it could also be another transport ship waiting to evacuate the Lunar Base. The Lunar Base, with its many attached habitats, and a prison miles from there, still waits down on the moon for evacuation.

I think about it, and I don't believe a regular transport ship would be waiting behind the moon, on the opposite side from the base. It would be above the base, on this side. So, this has to be Devon.

Okay Kaci, think. No comm system. Fuel cells almost dead. So, do I head for Lunar Base and land, or head for the ship and hope it's Devon? And that I can make it that far? And that they will see me? I check all my sensors again. I can see back at Earth, the ship with Abishai on it has taken off. It is making its way out of the atmosphere. Good. At least he's now safe, and the Project has started. I also see the massive habitat ship slowly making its way around to this side of Earth to meet up with the transport ship and the rockets full of gold. It will be visible to everyone soon. I guess that's one less secret I'll have to keep. Dr. Kincaid must be ready to make his intentions known now that he knows the Project is successful.

I look back at the transport ship hiding behind the moon and notice something strange. It is moving away from its position slowly, keeping the moon as a shield from view of the Earth. Now I know this has to be Devon. He is trying to stay hidden from Dr. Kincaid. He must've noticed the giant habitat ship as well.

I alter my course and head toward the ship. I'm sure the Lunar Base has been attempting to reach me on the comm, but of course I can't answer.

I'm alongside the moon when my power fails. I still have emergency lights and life support for now, but my engines are dead. My momentum should carry me close enough for Devon to at least notice me. I hope.

Alone here in my ship, the loss of Abishai washes cold over me again. It was just hours ago that we were together, flying all around the Earth dropping the drones. Laughing. Kissing. Planning a normal date.

A serious of beeps warn me that I only have about thirty minutes left of life support. Okay, Devon. Now would be a great time to come get me. I am literally betting my life that it is Devon piloting that transport ship and that he will notice me in time.

The sensors show that the momentum is carrying me the right direction, but is it enough? The view out my window now is of the star field beyond the moon. The stars are usually such a comfort to me, but right now they just look cold and so far away.

My emergency lights start flickering, and my console goes dead, leaving me in the dark. No sensors. No engines. No Abishai. I'm totally helpless, floating in space. This really sucks.

I hear the life support system hiss to a stop. It will only take a few minutes to use up all the oxygen. As I drift off into unconsciousness I feel a jolt. It must be the lack of oxygen, I'm hallucinating. I wonder if I hit something. I can't keep my eyes open any longer.

CHAPTER 19

Rescue

I wake with a horrible headache. I realize I have survived somehow. Despite the pain, I'm very happy to be waking up at all. My head feels like it's stuffed with cotton, and my limbs are heavy. I look around and it's obvious that I'm not in the Celeste anymore. I sit up slowly and see that I'm in a small medi-bay. There are two empty beds on either side of mine. Automated diagnostic equipment above every bed. Clean and sterile. Transport ships typically don't carry doctors on every trip, but they do always have a fully stocked medical bay. This one looks like all the others I've seen. Transport ships are all designed and built the same. The identical designs supposedly provide comfort to the people traveling in them, which is important since they are the transition from Earth home to space habitat home.

So, how did I get here? Is it Devon that rescued me? Is this the Excelsior V?

I swing my legs off the table and carefully stand up. I feel like my body ran a marathon without me. I have to sit back down. Muscle weakness—and grief—weigh me down.

The door to the bay opens up and a familiar voice says, "Good ,you're up. Now maybe we can get some answers around here." A warm laugh.

I look toward the door. "Devon. Thank goodness." Then, "What took you so long? I was almost space junk out there." I try to smile, but my heart just isn't into it. My smile probably looks more like a grimace.

I look around to see if there is anyone else in here with us. Between the crying and the almost dying I must look as horrible as I feel. I shift self-consciously on the bed.

"Don't worry. We're alone. Everyone is busy getting your ship settled in the transport hold. I got you out of your ship myself." He gives me that big beautiful smile. "I got to you just in time, it seems."

"Thank you, Devon. Again you were there for me. I was hoping it was you waiting behind the moon. I was out of oxygen..."

Devon steps next to the bed and gives me a warm hug. I lean into him for support, my arms pinned to my sides. I listen to his heartbeat as he rubs my back.

"You're welcome, Kaci. I told you to trust me. Now, tell me what in the world is going on and what happened to your ship." His grip tightens around me, and he's trembling. He disobeyed orders in order to save me. I know now, that I need to trust him.

I fill Devon in on what happened. He knows some of it already, more than Dr. Kincaid realizes. Before Dr. Kincaid found Abishai and me in his ship, I had already updated Devon on the situation up to that point. He's part of my team, and most recently my friend, so I made sure he knew what we were facing down there. I had no idea the situation was going to get as serious as it did, though. I even tell him about Abishai and me.

I make him swear not to tell anyone and stress to him just how psycho Dr. Kincaid really is. Abishai's life depends on us not saying anything. As far as anyone else will know, I helped the good Dr. Kincaid finish his Eugenesis Project and my ship was damaged in the process. I'm not quite sure what to do about that last nuke we didn't find. When my head clears, I'll need to figure something out about that. In the far recesses of my mind, there is a small grain of hope that one day I will get Abishai back, too.

Although Devon doesn't like the idea of not telling our team, or his father, he promises me he won't say anything, for now. It's a relief to know that he hasn't reverted to his old attitudes. Even the Misfits are being nice to me. Devon tries to keep his distance from me, ever since I told him about my feelings for Abishai. I appreciate that he values our friendship enough to not push me. My heart aches enough without having to worry about hurting Devon's feelings.

Our transport ship is the last one around Earth, so we are enlisted to help the Lunar Base evacuate all their people and equipment. Somehow, Devon has managed to make his disobedience look like it was all planned, that the Lunar Base requested us to stay. Amazing how he can always avoid getting in trouble.

I take a shower and change my clothes and mechanically go through the motions of helping. Time creeps by. Minutes and hours that I've been away from Abishai. I try to focus on the simple tasks in front of me, to keep my mind from falling apart. Devon keeps me busy flying the shuttle back and forth from the moon to the transport ship. We bring up the last of the people and science habitats on this side of the moon. The only structure on the other side is the old prison. From here it looks like a dark bubble protruding from Luna's side.

We leave the long term monitoring equipment built into the moon. This equipment is aimed at Earth and has long term maintenance bots to keep it working. We will be able to watch the Earth for several generations at least. Even though all of humanity is leaving this solar system soon, we can monitor how the Eugenesis Project is progressing. No one alive today will be around to see Earth's complete renewal though; it will be centuries before humankind returns to Sol system.

The recycler barges join us, and we convoy away from the Earth and the moon for the final time. On our slow journey to Jupiter Station, the message is relayed to us that the Eugenesis Project is a success. Both serums have been successfully deployed. I make my way down to my ship, where she sits in the transport ship's hold. I lock myself in, climb into my familiar pilot's chair and cry.

CHAPTER 20

Routine

I take off my helmet, shake my sweaty hair out, and walk from the flight deck. I take the emergency maintenance ladder down one floor, instead of the elevator. If it were at all possible to avoid elevators altogether, I would avoid every single one of them. But on Jupiter Station, elevators are the only way to get around, except for the few maintenance ladders I've found. The elevators are just another reminder of Abishai. All the time we spent at the Compound in elevators and endless hallways. Stupid, I know, but I avoid them whenever possible.

I have just come back from another scout ship training session, and I'm pleasantly exhausted. After Command found out that I successfully helped Dr. Kincaid complete the Eugenesis Project, I was guaranteed a spot on one of the scout ship crews. Devon also made it. He was the hero at Lunar Base. We are again on the same training team, but this time I don't mind. Devon is different, softer somehow, and I love flying the little scout ships. I miss the Celeste, but these ships are smaller, faster, and built for long distance exploration. Exactly everything I have worked so hard for. If it weren't for the giant hole in my heart left by the loss of Abishai, my life would be perfect.

Devon and I spend a lot of time together. We hang out at meal times, go to the gym, and of course train together. It's nice having a friend to talk to, and he's the only one who knows my secret. All these years I missed out on a lot of social activities, so Devon is helping me make up for lost time in that area. He makes it easy for me to fit in socially, and it keeps me busy. He's as popular as ever, but still makes time for me.

I shower and change and then head down to my room to study. As a Scout, I have to learn about more than just space junk. I'm learning about retrieving raw materials, astronomy, geology and chemistry. My head hurts just thinking of all the chapters I need to read tonight.

I smile as I think about my history homework. I have taken an interest in Earth history and its many cultures, ever since meeting Abishai. But now, it's more than just learning about history in general. I'm learning about Abishai's family history. After I returned from Lunar Base, an absolute emotional wreck, I pulled myself together and decided I would find a way to help Abishai, somehow. So I enrolled in an African Earth history class. I love studying about the cultures that formed Abishai's mother's world. There are many habitat ships that represent each of the African countries, and I hope to discover someone who knew Abishai's mom. While I try to figure out how to help Abishai, this feels like, in some small way, that I still have some sort of connection to him.

I also watch the holo vids whenever Dr. Kincaid is on. Usually he's giving some sort of political speech or explaining how successful his Project has been. I don't care about his words. I hate him. I can't stand to see his face, but I hope to get a glimpse of Abishai. So far, he has never been seen with Dr. Kincaid. Dr. Kincaid hasn't even mentioned his son. Each time I see Dr. Kincaid, but not Abishai, my stomach tightens and I get a sick, sick feeling. I hope Abishai is all right. I haven't done or said anything to hurt Dr. Kincaid's political ambitions and neither has Devon. Dr. Kincaid just gets more powerful, and although that makes me nervous, it gives me hope that Abishai is still alive.

I finish the assignment for my elective college homework and put my books aside. My high school graduation is tomorrow. Our whole class decided to work toward an early graduation. We want to graduate before the Migration. We are going to be the last graduating class at Jupiter Station, where we have lived our whole lives. After graduation we will all go separate ways, be assigned to different habitat ships and jobs. We'll be scattered among the two hundred and fifty habitat ships that make up the Migration to New Earth. Jupiter Station will be left only as an unmanned outpost. It will connect with Lunar Base and relay information to us as we head out of the solar system.

A message comes in on my comm, and I see that it is my college history teacher. He wants to see me in his office. I tingle with excitement, although I try not to get my hopes up. My history teacher knows I'm looking for news on Abishai's mom. He doesn't know the situation with Dr. Kincaid, or why I need to find her, but I had to enlist his help so he could get me access aboard the habitat ships and their crew logs. I lock my quarters and head down to the Ed wing. Five elevators to endure.

I've learned that each of the Migration habitat ships represents one of the countries from Earth. Or at least those countries that could afford to build a ship, or combine with another country. They feel this will help preserve the cultures and histories. A year ago I couldn't have cared who the people were or how they were organized, but Abishai changed my whole mindset.

I've chosen to do my final paper on Habitat Botswana. I was drawn to their colorful culture and artwork, which remind me of the murals and artwork in Abishai's apartment. The colors, the murals of happy dancers, and the rich hues of the people and their clothing. It seems like it was forever ago that I was in that apartment with Abishai, instead of the weeks it's really been.

Dr. Zaman himself is from another of the African countries, Kenya. He has lived in space most of his life, but still has retained a thick accent and an affinity for wearing his colorful tribal clothes. He is my all time favorite teacher.

Today he is wearing a long, bright red and orange flowing outfit. It makes me smile.

"Hi Dr. Z. You want to see me?"

"Yes, Kaci. Have a seat please." I can't tell by his expression if this is good news or not. He keeps his face carefully neutral.

I sit down and wait. Maybe it's about my grade so far. This is an elective class, so I shouldn't be worried whether or not I'm getting a good grade or not. Being who I am, of course I expect perfection from myself, so I do worry.

He sits down behind his desk, relaxes with his finger tips pressed together. He does that when he's thinking. Great. I just want to get this over with.

"There is someone who wants to meet you, Kaci." He meets my eyes, and I can't help but relax a bit under his confident gaze.

I'm trying not to get too excited. It could be another dead end. Not knowing what Abishai's mother's name is has kind of made it hard to look for her. It seems there were a lot of African women who were transported off Earth the same year Abishai's mom was.

"It is a lady from Habitat Botswana." I sit up straighter in my chair. "She has requested that you go to her ship to visit with her. She has seen your draft essay and has some comments for you. I know we've had some bad leads, but at least this way, even if she doesn't have information on who you are searching for, you will at least get some good firsthand information for your paper." His face lights up in a wide grin.

Wow. "That's amazing. I've never had someone ask to see me about my paper. I've been the one requesting time from them to talk. This is good, right?"

"It is not unheard of for this kind of interest in one of my students. Our class is highly valued as a way of preserving history, even as we move away from Earth. I do suspect it might also have to do with your celebrity status on the holo vids. Maybe she is curious about the girl who saved the Project. It won't hurt to just talk to her, whether or not she is who you're looking for."

"Okay, I'm up for it. Just give me her habitat's location, and I'll take the Celeste over there right now. I need to take my ship on a final run anyway before I need to store her away." I feel sadness wash over me, as I am reminded of having to part with the Celeste. During the Migration, I will be flying a scout ship, so she will need to be put into storage on one of the habitat ships.

I get the location codes from Dr. Z and thank him for his help. I promise him an update as soon as I get back.

I head down to the Celeste. I think about the last time I flew her, and I'm again overwhelmed by the loss of Abishai. The memories of Abishai and me flying over Earth together are still so vivid. I haven't set foot in my ship since I was brought back from Lunar Base. Devon took care of making sure they repaired the comm and fuel cells.

That reminds me that I should probably let Devon know where I'm going. I will be missing out on our daily workout.

I swing by his quarters, but he's not there. Probably at the gym already. I leave him a comm message and head back to the docking area.

I enter the Celeste and am grateful that I'm alone. My emotions spill all over the place. I strap myself into the pilot's seat, program in my destination, and request to leave dock. I send a quick message to the Habitat Botswana ship to let them know that I'm on my way.

Pre-flight check done, I work on mentally pulling myself together. I remind myself, for the thousandth time, that even though it hurts to be away from him, at least Abishai remains alive. I somehow think that if he wasn't all right, I would know it. So I find comfort in this. I then concentrate on how good it feels to be behind the controls of the Celeste again.

Once out in the open, I enjoy the power and serenity of being in space. I love this part. The habitat ships are spread far apart between the planets, to avoid collisions or accidents; or rivalries. So I have lots of room to maneuver. The habitat ship I need to go to is stationed near Saturn. I rest back in my chair. My sensors are functioning properly, as well as the comm and fuel cells. I keep an eye on the life support. I know it's fine, but after cutting it so close the last time, I guess I'm a little paranoid now.

I get closer to Habitat Botswana and see that she is a beautiful ship. Her design is very different from the other habitats. Something about it looks familiar to me, but I'm not sure why. Her design is sleek and resembles a giant stingray. The control room is a bubble on top where eyes would be. The body of the ship is the triangular shape of the stingray, complete with a long tail. She's not one of the largest ones out here, but I see a lot of private expensive-looking ships docked in bays all around her. I get a signal from their control room where to dock, and I head down.

I squeeze carefully between two ships that are twice the size of the Celeste. They are of unusual design as well. They are graceful and similar to the scout ships I fly now. I dock carefully and prepare to board.

CHAPTER 21

Astrid

I leave the Celeste and find an escort waiting for me.
Good, I would get lost in this ship. Most of the habitat
ships I've been aboard are laid out all the same, in order
to make mass producing them easier, but not this one.
The uniqueness of this ship has me all turned around.

My escorts are wearing uniforms, but not the gray one-
piece kind that they wear on Jupiter Station. These uniforms
are multi-colored and fashioned quite differently. Even the
hallways are colorful. This is a nice change from all the white
hallways in the Compound as well as on Jupiter Station.

There are color coded stripes along the floor to give directions to different areas of the ship, and the lighting is pleasant, softer.

Finally, after being led down many hallways and elevators (ugh), we stop in front of a double door. The doors are opaque glass and as we enter, it feels more humid in here; a greenhouse. I have a sense of déjà vu. The ceiling is high, several stories tall to allow for the variety of tall trees. Underneath the trees a waterfall cascades into a pool, and a winding path disappears into the bushes. Very similar in design to the one at the Compound. I smile and close my eyes, as the familiar trees, sounds, and smells remind me of being with Abishai.

My escort breaks me out of my daydream and gestures to a woman sitting on a bench to my right. She is wearing a colorful dress with dark greens and bright yellows flowing all throughout the fabric. Her skin is the color of a cup of coffee with a touch of milk swirled in. I'm guessing she is about my mother's age. When she sees me, she smiles and beckons me over. I instantly like this woman.

I sit down next to her, and she takes both my hands warmly in greeting.

"Hello, Kaci. Thank you for coming all this way to see me. I don't get off the ship much, so I appreciate you flying over."

"You're welcome, uh Mrs...." Great. I can't remember what Dr. Z told me her name is.

"Oh, you can call me Astrid, Kaci." Her laugh is deep and rumbles from within her.

I smile, enjoying the sound of her laugh. "Astrid. It was no trouble, I love flying, and this trip wasn't that far."

"I bet you are wondering why I have requested you to meet me here?" Her hands are constantly in motion as she talks.

"Well, yes. Dr. Z, well, Dr. Zaman, hinted it might be because of the final paper I'm writing for his class." I frown. "I hope I haven't written anything wrong or offensive."

"Oh no, child! No, your paper was beautiful. It was written as if you actually had experienced our culture. Not just regurgitating something you read in a book. Very unusual for someone who has lived on Jupiter Station all her life." She tilts her head as if questioning me. Her deep brown eyes burrow into mine, searching. Her gold hoop earrings glint in the artificial sunlight.

I hesitate. I hear in her voice more than just a question. She knows something, but I don't want to get my hopes up again. My heart starts racing. I try to think past the web of lies I have constructed since meeting Abishai and try to come up with any truths I can share. "Well, I recently met someone who introduced me to this culture. So even though I didn't know him for very long, I immediately fell in love with the people in his stories and art." And Abishai. My stomach twists and knots in a tight lump.

She asks, still holding me firmly with her gaze, "And that was on Jupiter Station?" Crap, she's not buying it.

"Ma'am, I'm honored that you've invited to your ship. It's beautiful, and everyone I have met has made me feel comfortable. But, please, why have you really asked me here?" Dr. Kincaid's secret weighs me down like unwanted space junk, and the hope I'm trying to push to the back of my heart is about to explode out of my chest.

"Oh, Kaci. I know you don't know me well enough to trust me, yet. I can understand that. Let's take a walk. I have something to show you." She smiles a big, warm smile, grasps my hand and leads me down the pathway farther into the trees. The undergrowth here is thick and healthy looking. Green ferns and tall red and orange flowers line the pathway.

The ground under the ferns is covered with some sort of creeping ivy with dainty purple flowers. I even hear birds. Just like the ones in the greenhouse that Abishai and I spent time in. I wonder if they were able to save that greenhouse and take it all up to the habitat ship. Would Dr. Kincaid think of that? Maybe Abishai insisted. I hope so.

Judging by how far we have walked and the thickness of the forest around us, we end up pretty much in the center of the greenhouse.

"Beautiful isn't it Kaci?" Astrid has been watching my face as I marvel at the scenery around me. I should be nervous, here alone with a stranger, in the middle of an unfamiliar ship. But for some reason, I'm not afraid. I look right back into her rich brown eyes, and I see some sort of familiarity, comforting and curious at the same time.

"Yes, it is very beautiful. We have a greenhouse on Jupiter Station that I spent a lot of time in. This one is far bigger and more beautiful than ours, as well as very similar to another one I visited recently." Dang it. My eyes are full of tears. I look away. Don't cry.

"You mean the one you visited on Earth, with Abishai?"

I whip my head around and stare at her with my mouth gaping. Her expression is mischievous. How on Saturn's Rings could she know about that? My heart is beating so hard I think it will burst out of my chest. My skin goes cold with fear.

"How do you know?" I'm shaking now. All this time I've been hoping to find someone who knew Abishai's mom. "I haven't said anything about that to anyone. Only one other person knows about Abishai, and he would never, ever say anything." The tears have betrayed me and are falling down my face silently.

Astrid hands me a tie-dyed cloth handkerchief. I smile at the beautiful colors as I take it and wipe away my tears. Who uses these anymore?

"There now, child. It's all right, you can trust me. I know more than you think about what you went through on Earth. I just needed to make sure you could still be trusted. Kincaid has a way of twisting people's loyalties. And don't worry, there are no listening devices here in this part of the greenhouse."

"How do you know Dr. Kincaid? And how do you know what happened on Earth? And about Abishai? And...wait." My poor little brain is finally making some connections. "You designed this ship, didn't you?"

"Yes." Her mischievous smile is back.

"You must have worked at the Compound, and you designed that monster of a habitat ship that Dr. Kincaid has built? That's why this ship looks familiar. It's the same basic design."

"Yes. Although that one was not supposed to be so massive. He always did have to overdo things." She pauses, patiently waiting for me to make the rest of the connections. I can feel there is still something missing, something vital for me to figure out.

I take a shot at trying to figure out the missing piece. "Okay, so you must still have some sort of contact with the Compound? That's how you knew I was down there with Abishai."

"Kind of. Let me start at the beginning, and then I will answer all of your questions." She laughs that wonderful deep sound again.

She pulls me over to a tall tree and we sit down onto the mossy floor. Sitting next to her amongst all this greenery makes this whole day feel like a dream.

"First of all, Kaci, I am Abishai's mother"

I am stunned speechless. When I came here, I was hoping she had known Abishai's mom or had heard of her. But now she's saying she is Abishai's mom. This is what I've been hoping for all these weeks, and now I can't think of what to say or do.

I think of all those colorful paintings and artwork that I fell in love with in Abishai's apartment. They all belong to this beautiful woman before me. Now all the colors and designs aboard this ship make sense as well. My heart feels like it is being squeezed by a giant fist. All these years and she was up here, alive. Abishai was right.

CHAPTER 22

Warm Hugs

Astrid, Abishai needs to know that you are alive."

Astrid shakes her head, sadly. "Kaci, you have experienced Robert's — Dr. Kincaid's wrath. He is so unbalanced, you know we can't jeopardize Abishai's life. I know you miss Abishai and fear for him, but Robert is very dangerous. It is better that Abishai thinks me dead or missing. Remember Robert still has his arsenal of Old World nuclear weapons."

"Yes, but we did disarm five of them. And how on Pluto's name do you know all this? About the nukes, about what happened to me down there? You've been up here on this ship the whole time."

She gives me a small smile. "Well, you know that I designed the Compound right?"

"Well, no, not really. I can see now that you designed the habitat ships, and I knew you designed the greenhouse and the NASA shuttle launch area. I didn't know you engineered the whole Compound."

"Yes. Back in those days, Robert was still struggling to make his own place in the scientific world. His father was a scientist before him. In fact his father is the one who discovered and implemented the Polymer Bacteria." She is studying me now, her expression very serious. She again patiently allows me to grasp the big picture.

"Oh no! It was Abishai's grandfather who caused that?"

"Well, humanity had already pretty much destroyed the Earth. Overpopulation, destruction of natural resources, pollution. The bacteria was just the final step in the destruction." Astrid continues quickly. "But the bacteria was meant to reverse all the damage. Robert's father just didn't count on it mutating and destroying more than just what was it was designed for."

Horrified, I almost feel sorry for Dr. Kincaid. "So then Dr. Kincaid has been trying all these years, to make up for his father's failure, by creating the Eugenesis Project to reverse the damage to the Earth. No wonder Abishai continued to help his father out, even after he realized what Dr. Kincaid had done to you. Or what he thought he did to you." Astrid takes my hand in hers and just lets me think all this through.

I prioritize my thoughts and finally decide caution is the best. "Astrid, who knows you are here besides me? And do they know who you really are? And what about your family?" I pause for a deep breath. "Wait, first my original question, how do you know all about what I went through down there and about Dr. Kincaid's current plans?"

"Since I designed the Compound, I know all the security controls, access codes, and back doors into the systems." She lets go of my hand and stands up to pace. I smile. Just like Abishai does when he's thinking. "I have been connected all these years with the security systems. Video, audio, infrared. I have them connected to a small hand held computer I keep with me at all times. Now, the feed of course is useless, since even the Compound is destroyed by now." She gives a big sigh. "Which at least means Robert's Project is a success. But before, I watched as often as I could. I got to watch Abishai grow up, although from a distance. I do long to be able to hold him again." Her voice drops, and tears fall down her face.

"My family thinks I am missing just like everyone else does. Robert made sure everyone knew I 'left my son and disappeared'. My family is actually from Mozambique, not Botswana. My brothers, sisters, and my parents are all on the Habitat Mozambique ship. They have no idea I am here. As for the people on this ship, they took me in thinking I am a fellow Mozambican who lost her family on Earth. They have been very kind to me, so in return I helped design this ship and continue to work as their Chief Engineer. I enjoy it here, although I always miss Abishai and my family. The leaders aboard this ship will never side with Robert or his political motives, which helps me feel more secure here. Robert has bought many a vote on the Council. He also has control of my trust fund. When I went 'missing' my family had no choice but to release my accounts to him."

"That's horrible! You must be so angry at him for separating you from your son and family." My anger is starting to boil.

"And what use would that kind of anger do for me, Kaci? For Abishai's sake, I can't say anything. You know that.

141

You're in the same position. So if I stay angry all the time, it will only hurt me. That won't help anybody. I try to find good things daily to concentrate on, despite all that has happened. This greenhouse, for example. I have designed it to be a peaceful, soothing place to relax. And now I have you to be thankful for." She pulls me into a hug. Not just any hug, but a warm embrace that makes me feel loved and cared for and comforted.

"I am also thankful, Kaci, that you got to know my son, and that I finally have someone to share this heavy secret with."

"So is that why you had me meet you in the greenhouse? So no one will know why I'm really here?"

"Yes. Everyone here knows I love to come to this place and spend hours by myself. They just think I am sad from losing my family back on Earth. I wouldn't want to burden anyone here with the truth, even if I weren't so afraid of Robert. He has spies everywhere."

"Speaking of which, have you seen what he is doing with the new Council? Weaseling his way into power? Riding on his success with the Eugenesis Project. He won't stop at just a council seat."

"Yes, I have been monitoring the news vids, but what can we do? If it weren't for Abishai's safety I would've exposed Robert a long time ago. He doesn't deserve to have that kind of power. And he doesn't care who he hurts to get what he wants."

A thought wriggles to the front of my mind. "Do you have contacts or any feeds to his Habitat ship? Can you tell if Abishai is all right?" If I could just know that he is all right....

"No, unfortunately he built the ship after I left. I haven't had any success at hacking into his new security network."

"Now that there are two of us that know about Abishai, we can't just ignore this situation. That's why Abishai needs to be told you're alive. He finally came to the realization that it was his father's fault that you left, but there were many years that he blamed you for leaving. So he has all sorts of unresolved emotions. You know he kept all of your belongings. Your artifacts and murals are what helped me get to know him better and to learn more about your family history." She stops pacing and comes over to embrace me again.

We walk the myriad of paths in the greenhouse as she fills in the blanks about what happened before I met Abishai. I detail my experiences I had with him and tell her about his new projects and about how smart he is, how kind and caring. We end up crying and talking and laughing together for hours, there in the greenhouse.

Soon it is time for me to go. My next training class will start in a few hours, so I have to get back. I promise Astrid I will come back tomorrow to visit, under the same guise of needing more help with my paper.

As I depart, I feel like I'm leaving a part of myself again. Astrid, so warm and welcoming, like her son, has worked her way into my heart. I'm not used to all this love. For years I was closed off from everyone, except my mom; to avoid the hurt and pain after my dad died.

I have absolutely no idea what to do with all these feelings. Where do I go from here?

CHAPTER 23

Graduation

I get back to the station, and I go through the motions of going to classes, simulators, the gym. My head feels like it's in a fog. Devon has asked me several times what is wrong. I just tell him I didn't sleep well. I don't know yet if I should tell him about Astrid. Maybe later I'll decide to tell him.

As I get ready for bed, I realize that tomorrow is our high school graduation. How could I have forgotten? I message Astrid and tell her I forgot about my graduation tomorrow, but I will be by the day after, to visit with her. Graduation, which I looked forward to for so long almost seems insignificant after all I have gone through.

Graduation day finally arrives after a restless night of sleep. I have waited forever it seems to finally be done with high school, but all I can think of is Abishai and visiting Astrid tomorrow. I make it through the ceremony, but during the reception I start to get emotional, and all the people packed into the reception hall are making me jittery. Thankfully, Devon comes to the rescue. He makes some excuse about taking pictures and leads me out of the room.

"Thanks, Devon. I really needed to get out of there."

"Welcome." Devon smiles and steers me toward the greenhouse. "You look very beautiful tonight, Kaci. I don't think I've ever seen you in a dress."

"Thank you, Devon. It feels strange to not be wearing a jumpsuit or workout clothes." I smile back.

"You know, out of everyone here, I would think you would be a bit more excited about this day. You worked so hard to graduate despite all the other classes you're taking." I see concern in his handsome face. His blue eyes are sparkling, and once again I am reminded why he is so popular.

"I know. I really am happy to finally be done with all this and that we both achieved our Scout assignments. Now at least my mom won't have to work so hard. She can join me on the Scout habitat." I try to smile.

"You don't sound so happy." Devon's stunning blue eyes are boring into me.

"I know. I'm sorry. I am grateful that I have everything I worked so hard for." I turn away. "But I still miss Abishai."

We have made it to the greenhouse, and as I step through the doors, I automatically take a deep breath of the fresh moist air. Thankfully, even our training ship has a greenhouse. This one is very small compared to the others, but I still enjoy coming down here.

"Is that why you have been so distant lately, Kaci?" Devon is walking close enough to me that our shoulders are touching.

"Probably. And the fact that it frustrates me not to be able to do anything for him." My hands are clenched in anger just thinking about Dr. Kincaid again.

Devon laughs. "I can only imagine how tied up in knots your pretty little brain has been trying to find some way to get back at Doctor...uh the doctor." There are a few people in the greenhouse, and Devon notices in time before he says the name out loud.

We duck through the trees to a more secluded area. I keep my voice down as I ask, "Aren't you upset he tricked us, lied to us, almost killed me, and is basically keeping Abishai and his staff hostages?"

"Yes, of course I am, Kaci. I also get angry every time I see him on the news vids telling his lies and making outrageous statements and getting away with it all. But we can't do anything, remember? I promised you I wouldn't say anything. And he's dangerous, so what could we do anyway?"

"I know, I know. I really do appreciate you keeping your promise, Devon. You have been such a good friend to me, and you know I don't have many of those." I smile and bump shoulders with him. We walk over to the small pond in the center of the greenhouse, and I sit down on a large rock at the edge of the water.

Devon sits down beside me. "You know, Kaci, I would like to be more than your friend. Finally, after all these years I've gotten your attention, in a positive way. Not because I was tormenting or competing with you." Devon grins and puts his hand over mine. "You know I'm so sorry about all that. I see things differently now. I see you differently. But

I'm probably too late realizing it, huh? Since you still have feelings for Abishai."

I squeeze his hand. "I also feel differently about you since our time on Earth. We went through quite an experience together. What we've shared in the last few weeks has been great." I make sure I look him straight in the eyes, when I say, "And I'm glad to count you as a friend."

Devon lets out a big sigh. "Even though I would like us to be more, I do understand. And anytime I can get away from crowds and spend time with you, well that is as good as an excuse as any."

"Really? I thought you loved being the center of attention."

"Sometimes, yes of course, but after a while I get tired of putting on a fake smile on for people who hang around me, just to boost their social status."

I laugh. "Well, you have nothing to worry about that with me. I so don't care about my social status."

Devon laughs and tosses a pebble into the pond absently. "It's good seeing you laugh again. You've been so serious and so far away lately. Especially the last day or so. What is going on, Kaci? It's got to be more than just missing Abishai. You've been dealing with that for weeks, then all of a sudden the last few days it seems something has changed."

I find myself nervously twisting the ends of my hair with my finger. I hate situations where I don't know what to do. I'm still not really comfortable with trusting people, or even having someone to talk to, other than my mom. These last few weeks I've found three people I cannot only trust, but enjoy talking with. Abishai is of course out of reach, but hopefully not forever. My chest constricts just thinking about him. Astrid is wonderful, but she is a day's space flight away. But Devon is right here, in front of me.

I turn to face Devon. "I want to be able to tell you. But I already burdened you with the secrets surrounding our trip to Earth. I appreciate your friendship, but I don't want to put you through even more."

Devon gives an exaggerated sigh. "I know you're new to this whole friendship thing, Kaci, but that is what friends do. They lean on each other, confide in one another. Burden each other. I'm right here, I'm your friend, and I'm asking you to tell me what is bothering you."

Devon grasps both my hands. His intense blue eyes dare me to trust him.

I smile. "Okay. But it is about Abishai."

He doesn't let go of my hands, but he does stiffen a bit. "I guess I kind of figured it would be, Kaci. I understand. I'm okay with just being your friend. Well, not just your friend, but your best friend, maybe." He gives me one of those million dollar smiles and lets go of my hands to give me a hug.

Relieved we have crossed that hurdle, we settle in side by side on the rock.

"I found Abishai's mom."

I can't help but laugh when I see the shocked look on Devon's face. I double check that we're still alone and tell Devon about how I found Astrid. I tell him how warm and caring she is, how talented of an engineer, and how she has monitored Abishai all these years.

After I finish, I try to wait for Devon to process it all. Unfortunately, I'm not as patient as Astrid.

I nudge him with my elbow, "Well? What do you think?"

"Wow. I can see why you've been so distant lately. That is a lot to process. Good grief, you wait until our grad night to tell me this?" He smirks and nudges me, and I nearly go flying into the pond.

He catches me before I fall in. "Whew! Thanks. The one night I wear a dress I almost get drenched. My mom would kill me if I came back to the party looking like a wet space rat." I smile, imagining that scene. "Although the look on her face would be priceless. Tempting, very tempting." We start laughing, knowing that I'm totally capable of doing something like that just for the satisfaction of my mom's reaction. I am, after all, the reason for her gray hair.

Devon stands up and pulls me to my feet. "Nope. We aren't going back to the party, Kaci."

"Why not?"

Without hesitating he answers, "We're going to start planning how to get Abishai back and hopefully fix Dr. Kincaid for good." He takes my hand and leads me out of the greenhouse.

I am shocked and let him drag me along the corridors.

As we stand outside the elevator, I turn to him. "Seriously, Devon? After all this time, you think we're going to be able to come up with a plan? One that will keep Abishai safe and keep Dr. Kincaid from using nuclear weapons? Are you crazy?"

"Yep."

"Okay. And where are we going?"

"The Celeste," he says, smiling mischievously.

"My ship? Why?"

"You're going to introduce me to Astrid. She has to be part of this. Now that we know someone else knows about Dr. Kincaid, I'm sure you can come up with a plan."

I hold the elevator door open. "What about our grad party? People will wonder where we disappeared to."

Devon shakes his head. "We can just say the best way to celebrate is to fly. And you still have that paper to do that Astrid is 'helping' you with. Everyone knows how, uh well, overachieving you are. They'll understand." Devon gives a little laugh. Almost just a giggle. At my expense. He mashes the button to close the elevator door, and I can't think of a single retort.

I regret wearing this stupid dress now, as we run down corridor after corridor. I can't tell if Devon is more humored by my nerdy reputation, or seeing me running in a dress.

"Can we at least stop at my room so I can change?" I caught a glimpse of myself in a passing glass door, and now I'm giggling too. My mom would say this is very, very un-ladylike.

"Nope. It's not like we're going to go sneaking around tonight. We're just planning. Right?" This excitement and purpose has given Devon a rush. He lives for flying and dangerous assignments. Just like me. All these years I thought we were so different, but when it comes down to what we're really passionate about, we aren't that different.

Breathless and still giggling, we reach the Celeste. Not changing was a good idea. Everyone we pass just thinks we are celebrating for graduation. Giddy teenagers. Devon looks handsome and stunning in his black and white tuxedo. Even while running. Of course his tie is long gone. I, on the other hand, feel very out of place, trying not to trip on my skirt while being dragged down the hallway.

In the Celeste we buckle in, Devon in the co-pilot's seat. I use the comm to call in our travel plan and send a message to Astrid. It's still before dinnertime, so hopefully she will be able to meet with us on such short notice.

CHAPTER 24

Planning

I enjoy every minute of the flight. No matter what seems to be happening around me, speeding through space, watching the familiar stars go by, is as near to being in heaven as I can imagine.

I dock with Astrid's habitat ship and give Devon a big smile. He, too, is in awe of the design of Astrid's ship. "Nice, huh? Astrid designed it and the giant one Dr. Kincaid built. Beautiful and functional."

I start to unbuckle from my harness. "I appreciate you doing this for me and for Abishai."

"Oh I'm just in it for the fun. And, you know, getting back at Dr. Kincaid." He nudges me with his shoulder, again sending me almost flying out of my half unbuckled harness. He apologizes while laughing and helps me up.

"Okay, save the show of muscle strength for later." We head for the hatch.

Again, we have an escort. They eye Devon warily, but I assure them he's a friend of mine. I give what I hope is my most trustworthy smile.

This time our escorts lead us down to the engineering section. Astrid is up to her elbows in electronic parts and pieces in some sort of machine I don't even recognize. "Hi, Astrid."

"Hello, Kaci! I was surprised when I got your message that you would be coming today." She smiles and looks me up and down. "I thought you had your graduation today. Sure looks like you're still dressed for it."

I laugh. "We did. This is my friend Devon, who I told you about." He gives her a little bow and one of his charming smiles.

"I am delighted to see you both. Let me just put this darn thing back together." Quickly she puts all the pieces and parts back into the mystery machine.

She washes her hands and gives me one of her motherly hugs. I melt into it, enjoying feeling loved. She even gives Devon a hug. He looks sheepish afterward. I warned him she was friendly. Maybe his mother doesn't hug him enough either, cause he's now smiling like a happy puppy.

After finding out that we didn't stay for the grad feast, Astrid takes us back to her apartment so we can have a meal together. Her apartment is of course colorful and inviting, just like the one down on Earth. The designs in the murals and tapestries are slightly different, but still colorful. Lots of reds, yellows, and greens on the walls, floors, and furniture.

Astrid makes us a wonderful meal. We eat in silence at first, enjoying the food. I've been so used to grabbing quick meals out of the synthesizer, that this real food is a wonderful treat.

Astrid breaks the silence with a sweep of her arm and says, "Kaci, so you know, I have specially designed dampers in my apartment, so we can talk freely."

"Oh, that's great, Astrid. Devon has been a good friend to me and has kept our secret about Dr. Kincaid this whole time. I told him about meeting you and who you are. I hope that's okay with you. I trust him."

"If you trust him, I'm all right with it. I'm just not used to having anyone to talk to about Abishai. I built the dampeners just in case. I always hoped maybe I could find someone I could trust." Her big brown eyes are tearing up, threatening to overflow.

"Astrid, Devon and I came over so soon because we have a plan." Looking over at Devon, "Well, more of a plan to plan."

"A plan for what, child?" She starts to clean up the dishes, and I stand up to help her.

"A plan to get Abishai back."

The dishes she is holding crash to the floor. I rush over and help her clean up the mess.

She sits down and allows me to finish cleaning up the floor. "What? What are you talking about?"

Devon answers for me. "There are three of us now who know about Dr. Kincaid and Abishai. We should be able to come up with a plan. We can't just let Dr. Kincaid get away with this. We don't want this kind of person heading up the Migration. It's more than just us that will suffer at Dr. Kincaid's hand." Devon's voice is tinged with anger now. "He has kept you away from your son for all these years, he almost didn't let me leave in one piece, and Kaci was barely alive when I finally got to her." He closes his eyes to calm himself down. When he opens them, his voice is calmer, "Kaci loves Abishai, and I am her friend, so we need to bring him back." He's looking at me now. I know that it hurts him to realize I won't love him the way I love Abishai. He has chosen to acknowledge that and to be a true friend to me. I am beyond grateful.

"Thank you, Devon." I give his hand a squeeze.

Astrid's voice filled the room. "Well, goooood night! I'm not sure what to think. Of course I would love to have my Abishai back, but Robert is not going to let us just go in and get him. And even if we somehow did get Abishai out of there, Robert would do anything to get him back. Abishai is his pawn to keep power over us. He always has been." She sounds nervous and sad, but I can see a glint of hope in her eyes.

"Astrid. I think we can do this. Devon and I have been highly trained for dangerous missions. You are an engineering genius, and you know how Dr. Kincaid thinks. I think we all have the right kinds of gifts and knowledge, so that if we work together, we can do this." My words are coming out in a rush.

Astrid gets up and starts pacing the room, her flowing sari rustling wildly around her. "You know, your grad party is not the only celebration happening today." She is grinning widely. "The Council is also celebrating the countdown before the Migration. They will all be meeting tonight for a huge meeting and dinner party on the Council ship. Every council member, including Robert, has to be there. They will be voting on who will lead each phase of the mission. It would be the perfect time to get aboard his ship to look for Abishai."

I could just hug her. I am overjoyed that she has agreed to help, but tonight is so soon. I try to force the nerves out of my voice. "That is great! But tonight? I've been watching the vids and noticed that Dr. Kincaid has not left his ship much. He even vids into the Council meetings. Do you think he really will show up in person for this meeting? He tells the media that he has 'space sickness' and is still getting used to being off Earth. Personally, I think he is just nervous to leave his ship because he has Abishai hidden there. He is very paranoid."

"Yes, he has to go in person. The Council has mandated it. I have a few connections that tell me that they have stepped up security around the Council ship so that all the members will feel safe coming. Up here in the habitat ships, we have lived all these years without any sort of fighting or fear of safety. I'm afraid the last few countries that have come to live in space the past three years, have made the political scene not so peaceful. So there is extra security. If the leaders want to retain their Council seats, they have to be there in person tonight."

Devon stands up. He comes over to where I'm standing with Astrid. "Today? Tonight? That doesn't give us much time to plan. Do they have any other meetings like this coming up soon?"

"No, they won't meet face to face again until right before the Migration leaves. This might be our only chance to sneak onboard his ship. Most of his security will go with him. I imagine he doesn't truly trust the Council's security." Astrid pulls out her palm computer and starts typing.

Devon continues with more questions. "Astrid, how do you know all this? How do you keep tabs on the Council if you're here on this ship as an engineer?"

"My family has great influence out here and a great relationship with all of the countries. Even though my family thinks I am dead, I still have a few loyal contacts that help me. They know me as Astrid, who was the personal attendant to the princess. On Earth, my parents were the king and queen of our country. Astrid was my constant companion, my personal servant, and my best friend. A few years older than me, she was very similar to me in likeness. That is why they chose her to serve me, as a body double. We were inseparable, like sisters. We would switch clothes sometimes, switch roles even. We fooled almost everyone when we were younger." Astrid's eyes are distant and she is smiling, thinking of her friend.

"When Robert forced me to leave, he had his guards kill her, to show me he was serious and in control." Astrid's shoulders slump, and I can see the sadness as it threatens to overcome her. "Since she looked just like me, I took her identity and ran. Robert wouldn't let me take Abishai with me. He threatened to kill our son if I tried to take him. My family just thinks that as Astrid, I'm too overcome with grief for my mistress, to join them on their ship. They allow me to live here, but I keep in contact with a few staff on my family's ship that Astrid and I were friends with."

I give her a hug. So much sadness in her life, yet she can still smile and laugh and give someone like me her love. I pull back far enough to look her in the eye. "I'm so sorry about your friend. So if Astrid is not your real name, what is it?"

She smiles. "Amira. My name is Amira. It means Princess in our language. My father wanted to make sure everyone knew my destiny." She is beaming now. "It feels good to say it among friends again. I have been Astrid so long, I have become her. I had given up hope of ever living my own life again."

Devon sits down. "Well, Amira, if we succeed in getting Abishai out of there tonight, you need to let your family know you're alive and become the Princess again." With tears streaming down her face she grabs Devon back up in a three way hug. Finally she lets go of us, and we head over to the table sit down and start planning.

CHAPTER 25

Disguise

Okay, Amira since you seem to know Dr. Kincaid's schedule, do you have any ideas how we can get the three of us in?"

She uses her small computer to project a three dimensional picture above the table. It shows Dr. Kincaid's giant habitat ship. "He should be leaving in about an hour for the Council ship. His commuter ship is here." She points to a dock on the underside of the habitat. "All the docks are underneath, where the belly of the stingray would be. His commuter ship is the only one on this side, for security reasons. Very paranoid as you have noticed. Anyway, all the maintenance and supply craft have docks over on this other side. That is where we will have to go."

"Won't their security recognize my ship, Amira?"

"Probably, so that is why we're going over in a supply ship. There are regular supply ships going between all the habitat ships. Everyone is finishing up all the trading of goods and services before the Migration. They will still be able to trade between ships on the way to New Earth, but it will be much harder since all the ships will be traveling at such high speeds. We need to be pretty much self-sufficient." She focuses the projection underneath the habitat, where the supply ships dock. "There is a supply shuttle leaving from our ship in two hours with cases of ethnic food and crates of special parts for Robert's ship. The parts, which I designed, will boost the life span of his solar power cells. He has purchased five hundred of them." She graces us with her hearty laugh. "If he knew it was me designing them, he would never have purchased them. He would think I had them sabotaged."

"Have you? Sabotaged them I mean?" I can see on Devon's face that he had the same question.

"Oh no, I would never do that. I build these for all the ships. It is one of this ship's chief exports. Keeps me valuable here." She winks, and I smile.

"Okay, Amira, we take the supply shuttle over and then what?"

"Devon and I will stay with the supply ship. We will help unload the parts. That will allow me, with Devon's help, time to get access to their security system. From within the ship I think I can disable the security and help you locate Abishai. I'll get Devon one of the maintenance uniforms to blend in. They all know me so they won't pay any attention to me."

"Sounds good. What about me?"

"You are going to find Abishai and bring him back to the shuttle."

I shake my head. "They won't just let me walk in there and take him. They'll recognize me, and besides, I imagine he is well guarded as well."

"Don't you worry, I have a few more tricks up my sleeve, girl. I'll borrow one of our Chef's steward uniforms. You will be delivering food to the 'prisoner'. Knowing Robert, I am certain that they have Abishai locked up somewhere separate from everyone. He wouldn't be trusted to just walk around the ship." Amira looks me over. "Looks like we will need a good disguise for you. You spent enough time down there that they'd spot you in no time."

"Umm....maybe a hat?"

"Nope. Now we go visit a few of my friends. They will help us with our disguises and get us the equipment we need." She heads toward the door and Devon and I follow. When this woman puts her mind to something, she really rolls with it. I like her a lot.

We follow her down to the belly of the ship. The first friend of hers we meet is the Chief of Stores. He has access to all supplies on the ship. Amira is a genius and well connected.

After Amira introduces us, she sends Devon off with the chief to get supplies we will need. She then leads me up to the ship's stylist. Yes, a hair stylist.

I walk into the salon, and all I can manage to say is, "This is different." I'm staring at shelf upon shelf of wigs and hair extensions flowing along the whole back wall of the shop. I turn to Amira suddenly nervous, "I just usually go to the barber shop and get my hair trimmed so it doesn't get stuck in my helmet. I don't know if you noticed, but I'm not really a frilly type girl."

"Now is as good a time to start, Kaci. Besides we need to radically change your appearance, so they don't recognize you." She laughs and walks over to a woman who looks like she just stepped out of a fashion holo vid. Tall, slender, with darker skin even than Amira. She is wearing a tight gold and orange glittering outfit. Her skirt stops right above her knees, and her top is lacy and almost see through. Not quite the type of outfit to go for a space walk in. I imagine her trying to get a space suit on over that dress and end up almost giggling out loud.

They have a hushed, animated conversation, while I look at all the wigs on display. Both women are gesturing wildly with their hands, and I can't help but smile. Model lady walks over to me and looks me over like she is trying to take me apart. Amira is right behind her smiling at me.

"Kaci," says Amira, "Tara here is going to take good care of you." She smiles and gives me a quick hug. As she starts toward the door, I look pleadingly at her as she is backing out of the salon. But she just keeps going. "It's okay Kaci, we decided we can't just use wigs, they are too easy to discover. Tara will fix you up good. No one will be able to recognize you when she is done." She takes another step out the door, smiling wickedly. "I have to go to make sure the supplies and tools are ready." Then she is gone.

An hour later I have had my hair washed and dyed, cut and styled. Tara has done my makeup, and now someone else is doing my nails. These ladies sure can do a lot to you in such a short amount of time. I haven't seen myself yet, but I think my hair has been dyed blond. I sure hope this all works. I can't believe the girls at school endure this willingly.

Amira comes back carrying a white uniform in her arms. She lets out a loud squeal when she sees me. Then she is laughing and crying at the same time. Crap. Is it that bad? I scramble out of my chair in the corner and run toward the closest mirror. I'm thinking from Amira's response, Tara has made me into some sort of freak of nature.

I slide to a stop in front of the mirror, and my jaw drops. Honestly, I didn't even recognize myself. I have never worn makeup or done anything with my hair like this. I see in front of me a pretty girl with beautiful straight blond hair that moves and feels fabulous. The makeup, which I expected to look sleazy on me, actually looks great. I look beautiful. I'm speechless.

I turn around just in time to be snatched up in a giant bear hug from Amira. She finally lets go, and then Tara and Amira are chattering and laughing and crying about how good I look. That's when I hear a crash behind us. All three of us whirl around.

There stands Devon in the doorway. He has dropped his bags of equipment and is staring open mouthed at me.

I instantly feel my cheeks grow hot and know that I'm probably blushing bright red.

Beside me, laughing hysterically again, both Amira and Tara are doubled over and pointing at Devon. Amira finally finds her voice amongst her giggles, "Look at that boy's face! Tara I think you've outdone yourself. Devon you might want to roll up your tongue and put it away now. Might be hard to walk with your jaw hanging open like that." She snorts and I can't help but join in with their laughter.

Devon now turns a few shades of red too. Good, glad I'm not the only one. "Uh, well, Kaci you look amazing! Sorry for staring. I've just never seen you done up like this."

I'm still giggling, I can't help it. First of all, it's nice to feel pretty. Secondly, Devon looks like he's really regretting being just my friend.

After the laughter dies down, an awkward silence pervades the room. I think we're all collectively thinking, now what? Amira to the rescue again. "Okay, Kaci now go in the changing room and put this uniform on." She's still grinning insanely, and I can't stop either. I try to calm down by reminding myself, that this is all to rescue Abishai. That even though it's been fun being pampered, and I have enjoyed the laughter, this isn't just a fun day at the salon with the girls. There's a reason I have to change my looks.

I put the white uniform and hat on and allow Tara to adjust my hair around my face and the hat. I look in the mirror and my reflection looks much older than seventeen. I'm pretty sure no one will recognize me now.

Devon and Amira pick up the equipment that was dropped. Devon has already changed into his maintenance uniform and keeps glancing over at me. I walk over to him, noticing that he looks very handsome in his uniform. "So Devon, do you think they will recognize me at all?" I'm trying to keep a straight face. I imagine I look older that way, but it's too hard to do right now, and I end up in giggles again. "Devon?" This time I punch him in the arm.

"What? Yes, no. Good grief. Yes, I think you look great, and no I don't think they will recognize you."

"Okay children, let's go." Amira is heading for the doorway. "Thank you, Tara again for all your help."

"Yes, thank you Tara." I give her a quick hug and head after Devon and Amira. If I live through this mission I promise myself to come back and visit her again. It's nice feeling pretty, and besides, I will eventually need her help to get my original dark hair back.

We arrive at the shuttle and stow away all of our gear. We find that the kitchen has sent several cases of food for me to deliver. Thankfully they are loaded on an anti-grav pallet, so I'll just have to push it along the hallways. They have left hidden empty spaces in the cart for me to hide some tools and gadgets I will need once I find Abishai. Thinking about him gets my heart racing. I can't believe we are actually doing this. I can't wait to see him again, and I hope he is all right. My stomach twists thinking of what Dr. Kincaid could've done to him by this time.

We strap in and release from the dock. It's very strange to not be flying the ship. I look over at Devon, and it looks like he's thinking the same thing. When you're used to being in control, it is unnerving just being a passenger.

Even Amira is quiet for the ride to the other ship. Devon and I have been careful to only call her Astrid when others are around. Once again, I am overwhelmed with all the wonderful people that are in my life now.

CHAPTER 26

Captive

My nerves kick in once we dock with Dr. Kincaid's ship. My stomach is a tight little knot and my hands are sweaty. I hate how much Dr. Kincaid scares me. Devon reaches over and squeezes my hand and gives me an encouraging smile. Grateful for his friendship, I return the squeeze. He pretends being grossed out by my sweaty hands, and I can feel some of the tension drain from me. I smile as the shuttle docks, and the doors open to the other ship's cargo bay.

Amira comes over and gives us whispered instructions on where to go. Devon will stay with her in this bay, and I'll head up with the food. She slips me a communicator to place in my ear.

"See you soon, Astrid." She smiles and hurries off to the far side of the bay. She will hack into the ship's computer while Devon unloads and distracts the crew here.

I nod to Devon and head over to the elevators. I won't know where to go yet, until Amira gets into the computer. For now I will head toward the kitchen deck and try to blend in and act like I know where I'm going. I walk through the hallway and see several people that were on Earth with Dr. Kincaid. As I pass each one, my pulse quickens, but they don't seem to recognize me. It looks like he has increased his crew with others from somewhere, since there are a lot of new faces. I'm not sure where he could've picked up so many new people in such a short time, and I haven't seen anyone yet from Abishai's crew.

I walk slowly pushing the anti-grav cart. People in uniforms are coming and going briskly from this hallway with supplies. There are a few older men that smile at me, which creeps me out, but mostly everyone just goes about their business. Dr. Kincaid's team is on the lookout for a petite, feisty, brunette; not a beautiful, blond professional chef steward. I smile confidently as I move along.

Soon Amira has hacked into the computer and gives me directions through the earpiece. "Kaci, you need to head to elevator 10B just past the kitchen. Take it all the way up to Level 34. I'm sending messages to that floor to expect a delivery from the kitchen. I think they have Abishai there, because it's the only floor that has full security, even in the vent ducts. Wonder why he would do that?"

I giggle as I step into the elevator. No one is on this one, so I whisper back to her, "Because that is how Abishai and I broke into the secure area down on the Compound.

Apparently he used to do it all the time when he was little."

"Oh, well that makes sense then. Good thinking." I hear a smile in her voice. She's probably remembering Abishai as a child. My heart breaks for Abishai not being allowed to know this wonderful woman.

"Once you get in there, the only way to get him out of there is down the same elevator. I'm going to have to come up with some kind of plan. Let me know when you have him."

"Okay, will do." I straighten my uniform, just as the door whooshes open at Level 34, and I'm staring at two large armed guards. Ugh. One of them is the one that struck Abishai in the stomach on Earth. I look down, hoping that he won't recognize me. I feel like my heart is going to beat right out of my chest.

"Arms up, missy. You know the drill. Pat down time." Yep. Still the same jerk.

He pats me down, his hands lingering longer than necessary. They look all around the anti-grav cart supplies. I am stuffing my anger and nerves down; I need to stay calm. Stick to the plan. Get Abishai out first. Then deal with this jerk.

"All right you're clear to go, missy." I push the cart past them, my hands shaking.

Amira whispers in my ear, "Good job, Kaci. Stay calm and keep walking until you get to the end of the hallway and then take a right."

I'm so thankful to hear Amira's soothing voice. I take a deep breath and walk faster. There are many doors along this hallway, but I turn right as Amira said, and find another long hallway with only two doors this time. "Okay, here there are two doors," I whisper back.

"The one on the left. I still haven't been able to completely disable their security system so just keep playing along."

"Okay." I get to the door and it's locked. My heart starts racing again.

"Amira?" My voice comes out an octave higher than intended.

"Use the pass card the chef gave you. It should work for the door."

"Oh, right. Sorry."

I key myself in, push the cart in and quickly close the door. I turn around and check out the room. It's a small kitchen with a few chairs and bare tables. There are many boxes stacked against the walls. Obviously, this is not Dr. Kincaid's main kitchen area. This one is bare and has only one small food synthesizer. I push the car over to it and take my tools out of their secret compartments. Thankfully, the jerks didn't find them in their search.

I walk to the other side of the room where another door is. It is solid and has several locks on it; this has to be where they are keeping Abishai. Excited and nervous all at once, I fumble with my tools and end up dropping half of them. Get a grip, Kaci! You can do this. I check the kitchen door again, to make sure no one is coming and go back to working on the locks.

Finally, I get the locks open. "I have the locks undone, Amira."

"Good. I have disabled the alarm on that section finally. I am still working on an escape route."

I open the door and find myself in a room about twenty feet across and about the same deep. The lighting is very dim in here, but what light there is shows more boxes stacked everywhere. Great, another storage room? As my eyes adjust, I notice that the boxes in here are not stacked against the walls, like they were out in the kitchen area. They seem to be arranged in sort of a circle at the other end of the room.

"Abishai? Are you here? Abishai?" I'm frozen in fear that I have the wrong room, but I'm also afraid at the same time that this is the right room.

I hear a noise off to my left in the far corner of the room, on the other side of the boxes. Then a low voice. "Just leave it by the door. I am not hungry. Go away."

Abishai. His voice sounds weak. Something is wrong here.

I walk around the boxes, toward where I heard his voice. There is a light on back here, low to the ground. I come around a box and see him lying on a thin mattress. The light is beside him, and he has books strewn all around him. He looks very thin, and he's unshaven. His hair has grown long with the tight curls sticking out in every direction. "Abishai! What have they done to you?"

He looks up at me. His eyes are lifeless, he doesn't recognize me. "What do you want? I said to leave the food at the door. You should not be here talking to me." He turns away from me and curls up in a ball.

I step closer, kneeling down beside him. "Abishai it's me, Kaci." I look down and realize, I don't look like Kaci anymore. "Abishai, please. I've had my hair colored, I'm in disguise, but it's me, Kaci. Abishai?" I reach out to touch his arm, and he flinches.

"Abishai, please, what have they done to you?" I'm crying now. I hate seeing him like this. What do I do now?

He finally turns back toward me. He reaches his hand up slowly and rubs my hair in between his fingers. Just like he used to do on Earth. "Yes, Abishai, they dyed and straightened my hair. Remember, I used to be a brunette?" I'm smiling, hoping. He's staring at me with those awesome green eyes of his. The eyes I first fell in love with. I can see light coming back into them. He's trying to put it all together.

I practice Amira's patience and just let him play with my hair while his mind takes it all in.

"Kaci? Is that really you?" He's smiling now.

"Yes, Abishai." I lean closer and he grabs me in a bear hug. He's crying and hugging me tightly, and I hug him back with all my strength. I pull away a bit so I can see his face. "Abishai, what happened? You look like you haven't eaten in weeks, and why are you locked in this storage room?"

"It is a long story, Kaci. Basically, I refused be the perfect son he thought I would be, once you left. He could not control me, so he locked me up here. He thinks I will eventually come around to his way of thinking. But I will never, ever support what he is doing." His voice is bitter, angry, sounding darker than I have ever heard him.

"I'm so sorry, Abishai! We should have come for you sooner! I didn't know!" I'm crying even harder now. He wipes my tears away and kisses me firmly on the lips.

"I have missed you so much, Kaci! I never thought I would see you again! But he cannot find you here. You have to go. He will not hesitate to kill you." Fear is in eyes now, and he holds me at arm's length.

His fear turns to confusion. "Wait Kaci, what do you mean, we? There are others here with you?" He's trying to look around me.

"Yes, Abishai, they are down in the docking bay waiting for us. We need to go now. I'm going to get you out of here." I try pulling him to his feet.

"No, Kaci you have to get out of here. I cannot go with you." He has tears running down his face.

"Yes, you can, Abishai. We have a plan, trust me."

"No, Kaci you do not understand." He rolls up his sleeve and pulls the light closer to him. "My dear father implanted a detonation device in my arm. If I leave this floor, it will explode."

CHAPTER 27

Warm Soup

I swallow hard, as bile threatens to come up my throat. "Seriously? Crap. Oh, Abishai." I take his arm and look. There is an inch long scar, and I can feel a hard object underneath his skin. Crap. Crap. Crap.

He's shaking now, so I sit down next to him and hold him. "It's all right, Abishai. We'll figure this out. I am not letting you go again."

I call Amira on the comm in my ear. "Did you hear all of that? Can you believe what Dr. Kincaid has done? What do we do now?"

"Yes, child I heard." She's crying. "Let me think of something. I won't let him go again either. Give me a minute here."

"Okay, I'll get him ready to go and wait for you. I know we can figure this out."

"Thanks, Kaci. I'll go get Devon and we will get you two out of there. Just take care of my baby."

"I will. Thank you, Amira."

I turn to Abishai. His mouth is hanging open, and he has a surprised expression on his face. "Amira? The person who is helping you is named Amira?" The last few words I can hardly hear, as his voice is now a whisper.

I forget that he can only hear my side of the conversation. "Abishai this isn't how I wanted you to find out, but, yes, your mom is the one helping me. Your mom, Devon, and I came to get you. I found her a few weeks ago. It's a long story, but once we get you out of here, she can tell you her whole story. I have gotten to know her, and she is wonderful, and she misses you very much. She is also super smart, just like you remember her, so I know she will help us figure out how to get out of here."

His eyes are glazing over again. I pull him to his feet and hug him. "I know this is a lot to take in, Abishai. But I need your help so we can figure out how to get you out of here." He pulls away slightly and places his hands on either side of my head and kisses me again. I melt into him, not wanting ever to leave his embrace again.

We are interrupted by Amira calling me back on the ear comm. "Kaci, are you guys still all right? How is Abishai?" I smile and take the earpiece out of my ear and hand it to Abishai. "Here, talk to your mom while I make sure the guards aren't getting suspicious yet."

I walk to the door. I can hear Abishai crying and talking softly to his mom. My heart is so full of love for both of them. It makes me even more determined than ever to get him out of here. I peek out the door and see that no one is in the kitchen still. I sneak out into the kitchen and look out that door. No one there, either. Good. On my way back into the storage room, I grab the rest of my tools and pocket a knife from one of the silverware drawers. Just in case.

Abishai is crying, but smiling. He hands me back the earpiece. "Thank you, Kaci." He kisses me again.

I place the earpiece back in. "Okay, Amira I'm back. The guards are still by the elevator, but they will get suspicious soon if I don't get a move on. Do you have any ideas about the device in Abishai's arm?"

"There is no way to disarm, Kaci. You're not going to like this, but you will have to take it out."

Oh. Not quite what I expected. Well, at least I grabbed the knife. "All right, I will do it. Anything to get Abishai out of here. How do I do this without it exploding, or Abishai bleeding to death?" Bravery only goes so far. "And then how do I get him out of here?"

"I'll walk you through the removal of the device. You need to do a few things first. Go back into the kitchen. I can see the trigger for the detonator is at the elevator, so Abishai is safe leaving that room."

"Okay, we're heading out there now." I grab Abishai's hand and we walk to the door. He shields his eyes when we step into the brightness of the kitchen.

"First thing you need to do Kaci, is unload the innards of your grav cart." Huh? What is she talking about? I go over to the cart. Looking all around it, I see that behind the hidden holes, where I stored the tools, there are small, almost invisible hinges. I open it up. It looks big enough for Abishai to squeeze in.

"Found the box. You're a genius, Amira. Abishai should fit in there, especially since he's lost a lot of weight. It doesn't look like he's been eating much." I frown, thinking of how much he has suffered all these weeks.

I hear her intake of breath. "My poor child." She clears her throat as she collects her thoughts. "In one of the containers is a roll of towels. You will need those to keep him from losing too much blood. You will also need a knife and some alcohol."

I root around and find everything I need. I sit Abishai down next to the cart. I have moved the cart so he's hidden from the door, in case someone comes in.

"Okay. I'm ready, Amira." I smile at Abishai and clean his arm with the alcohol. "Trust me, Abishai?"

He kisses me on the forehead, "Yes. Absolutely, Kaci."

I follow Amira's directions and carefully cut open his arm and remove the device. I feel awful hurting him, but I try to do it as quickly as I can. I then place the device in a bowl of soup Amira had me warm up. Apparently she thinks this device is heat sensitive, so we hope this will keep it from exploding right away. I clean his arm with the alcohol and wrap it up tight with the towels. He's very pale now.

"Doing all right, Abishai?"

"I am now. Let's get out of here." He smiles weakly.

I place him in the grav cart hiding space and give him a bottle of water to drink. "Here we go."

I adjust my uniform and take a few breaths. "Amira, we're heading out. Are the jerks still at the elevator?"

"Yes, and they have been joined by another one. Be careful Kaci. We will be waiting for you at the bottom of the elevator."

I open the kitchen door and carefully push the cart out. I stop and adjust the settings on the cart to offset Abishai's weight. It needs to look empty.

Again my heart starts racing, and my hands are sweaty. I turn the corner and see the jerks talking to another guard. Just the sight of them makes me sick to my stomach. Amira is whispering in my ear, trying to keep me calm. I'm so nervous, I can't concentrate on her words, so I just allow her voice to soothe me.

I get up to the elevator and all three stand up and face me. I try to look relaxed. Keep calm, Kaci.

"Took you long enough." Jerk number one.

"Yeah what were you doing, sampling all the food first?" His laugh raises the hairs on the back of my neck.

I look over at the third guard and catch my breath. Caleb. Crap. Just my luck, he's going to recognize me for sure. I can't breathe. I wipe my sweaty hands on my uniform and keep my chin down.

Caleb takes a step toward me. "Have you been here before? You look kind of familiar." He's looking me over, confused. I imagine myself taking the knife out of my pocket and stabbing him in the heart. Figures that he would be Abishai's personal jailer here, after he betrayed him to Dr. Kincaid.

I picture myself in the mirror at the salon. Think beautiful model, Kaci. I smile and play with my hair with my freshly manicured fingers. I look down and say in my sweetest voice, "I don't think so. I would have remembered someone as handsome as you." I'm not used to the whole flirting thing, so I hope I'm not overdoing it. I'm trusting the work Tara did on my disguise to protect me.

Silence. All three of them are staring at me. Crap. I can't breathe, and my knees are about to buckle. I need to get out of here.

Caleb's comm buzzes. Not taking his eyes off of me, he answers it. "Caleb, here." He listens. "Fine. I'll be right there."

He gives me a big smile. Creepy. "Looks like I'm needed in the control room. We can ride down the elevator together." He opens the elevator doors and steps in. The way he says the word together makes my flesh crawl and a sour taste rise up in my throat.

I carefully push the cart in, trying to keep it as far from Caleb as possible. I'm worried Abishai will make noise. The alcohol won't numb the wound for long. He has to be in a lot of pain.

I stand along the back wall, between Caleb and the cart. I wish I could've put the cart between us. He moves over closer to me until his shoulder is touching mine. I concentrate on not throwing up as he says, "I think I do remember you. From the bar on the market barge, right? I bet you could be a model, like on the holo vids." He tries to touch my hair and I take a step farther away. I'm right up against the cart now, nowhere else to go. I thought I was bad at flirting, but this guy is just awful.

I look down. "Uh, thanks. I really like working in the kitchens though. All that model stuff isn't for me." I think I'm going to throw up.

As he's about to say something else, the elevator door opens. Relief floods over me, but then he flashes a big smile and moves closer to me. "This is my floor. Look me up the next time you visit that bar again, okay?" He's staring at me, and I return his stare. Realizing he's not going to get anything further from me, he backs out of the elevator. The doors close, and I slide down the wall and sit down hard.

Amira is talking to me again. She probably was this whole time, I just couldn't hear her for my heart beating in my ears. I shake my head to clear it. She is saying, "Good job, Kaci. Just hang in there. Almost down."

I stand up and brush off my uniform. I close my eyes and get myself back into the role of chef steward. The elevators open and Amira is there waiting for me, just like she promised. I am so relieved I could hug her, but I restrain myself, since there are people milling around. We just head toward the shuttle, pushing the cart with its precious cargo hidden inside. Devon is there and helps us load the cart into the very back of the shuttle.

"Thanks Devon." I give him a quick hug and go take a seat near the cart. I'm eager to get Abishai out of there, but we have to wait until we take off. Amira sits next to me, and Devon goes up front to make sure no one comes to the back.

It seems like forever before we take off. Amira tells me she restored the security and made sure there wasn't any trace of her hacking.

Finally we undock and are in space. Amira and I scramble to the cart and open the door. Abishai tumbles out, sweaty and pale. Amira grabs him up, gently hugging him to her, while crying quietly and muttering under her breath about killing Dr. Kincaid for hurting her baby.

Amira gets her bag of medical supplies and gets him fixed up as well as she can. His bleeding has stopped, but he has passed out from the pain. I place his head in my lap and wipe his forehead with a cold cloth. Amira is still silently crying and smiling and holding his hand. As much as I love and miss Abishai, I can't imagine the heartbreak that Amira has gone through almost losing her son.

I wonder if my mother ever loved me that much. Maybe she still does, but just doesn't know how to show it anymore. She has always held me at a distance emotionally. I think something inside of her broke when my father died. The tears I cry now are tears of joy for Abishai and Amira and tears of sadness for the times I missed out with my own mom.

CHAPTER 28

Going Home

Devon comes back and kneels down beside us. "How's he doing?"

"He has lost a lot of blood, but he will have good medical attention soon. My boy is strong; he will survive this." Amira is smiling bravely, trying to believe her own words.

Devon looks nervously toward the front of the ship. "Yeah, about that Amira. We just passed the Habitat Botswana. The pilot said it was on your orders. Why aren't we stopping? Where are we going?"

"We're not going back to the Habitat Botswana. I do not want them to get in the middle of Robert's revenge on us. They are wonderful people, innocent of what we are doing. I know that Robert will track us down eventually."

I look up from Abishai and ask Amira, "Then where are we going? Abishai needs medical attention soon, and won't Dr. Kincaid find us anywhere we go? He can track this shuttle easily. I'm afraid I didn't think further than getting Abishai out of there." Okay, now I'm officially starting to freak out. I really hadn't thought this far ahead. I'm still amazed we got Abishai away from Dr. Kincaid. But now what?

"It's okay, child. We'll get Abishai fixed up soon." Amira is giving me her familiar warm, motherly smile. It makes me relax, if only a little bit. Abishai stirs in my lap, but doesn't wake up as I change the washcloth. His curls are plastered to his head, and he is very pale. His bandage is soaked again.

"So, Amira, where are we going?" Devon asks, as he hands me another bandage for Abishai's arm.

"We are going to the Habitat Mozambique. It is time I go home, and it is the only way to be safe from Robert. My family will protect all of us."

Devon and I look at each other. Wow. As if we thought there weren't enough surprises in this day.

I turn to look at Amira. "What will your family do when they realize you're alive? It's been so long. Will they be upset you've been in hiding this whole time? I know my mom would be furious."

"Well, we will see child. We will see. No matter how they feel, I am still family and so is Abishai. I think once they hear my story, they will understand. Forgiveness is a trait my family is strong in." She starts to get Abishai ready for transport, while humming a song to herself. I wonder if she is nervous, or excited to see her family again. I can't even imagine meeting your family after so many years.

We strap Abishai onto a medical anti-grav cart. He is still unconscious, but Amira assures me again that they have excellent doctors on her ship. I hope so. I didn't go through all this just to lose Abishai again, especially not to a bleeding wound that I caused him. I know I didn't have a choice, we had to get him out of that ship, but I still feel horrible looking at all the blood he is losing.

While Amira is fussing around with Abishai I walk up front with Devon. We are nearing Habitat Mozambique. She is beautiful, more tubular in shape, with tribal designs etched all over her hull. A functional, as well as artistic habitat. There are ships docked all over the underside, making them look like strange legs underneath the giant cylindrical beast.

I turn to Devon. "Once again, thank you for helping out. I appreciate all you've done to help us."

He shakes his head. "I keep telling you Kaci, that's what friends are for. Besides, this way you owe me." He smiles and gently pushes a lock of blond hair out of my eyes. With all the running for our lives, sweating, and crying, my makeup is probably a terrible mess. Devon leans down and gently kisses me on my forehead. "Now let's get ready for our next adventure. We're almost there. This little reunion should be interesting." He smiles his amazing Devon smile and goes to his seat to strap in. I return to the back and join Amira and Abishai.

She is listening to her ear comm. I sit down and fasten my straps for docking. When she's done, she turns to me and says, "Robert's ship just registered an explosion. He is rushing back from the Council chambers." She pauses. "Apparently the soup got cold." She smiles, even though she still looks tired and worried. "I will need to meet with my family right away and explain to them what is going on. Will you stay with Abishai in medical?"

"Of course. It's going to be a long time before I will let him out of my sight again." I grin at her and reach over to squeeze her hand. She has her other hand on Abishai's arm. I know that it will be hard for her to be separated from him again, but she has responsibilities to take care of, so he will remain safe. So that we will all be safe. It occurs to me that we will be having to deal with Dr. Kincaid soon, and that doesn't scare me as much as it should. I think maybe with Abishai safe, we can deal with Dr. Kincaid more forcefully.

We dock with the ship, and Devon comes back to help me take Abishai to medical. Once outside the shuttle, we encounter more guards. There must be a dozen of them, and they are blocking our path. Apparently they don't like surprise visitors.

Amira steps forward and speaks to them confidently in her native language. As always, she is talking with her hands and several times motions over to us. Disbelief, then shock registers on all their faces. I don't know how much of her story she is telling them, but pretty soon they are stepping back to let us go. They bow down before her with one knee on the ground. I guess they believe her. Then they escort her down the hallway.

Two of the remaining guards motion for Devon and me to follow them. We walk quickly to an elevator, with Abishai in tow. This elevator takes us to the very middle of the ship. We step out, and there is a medical team waiting. They take Abishai and hurry to a room down the hallway. I try to follow, but one of the doctors steps in front of me. "You must wait here. You and that boy can wait out in the seating area." He nods toward Devon.

"No, I will not. I will stay with Abishai. Amira told me I could. I will not leave his side." I try pushing him aside again, trying to get into the room.

He grabs me by both shoulders and his voice raises an octave or two. "Amira? Amira, our Princess? It is true? She is alive then? I heard it was her, but the guards saw you came in with Astrid." His fingers dig into my skin.

I wince at the pain. "Yes, it's really Amira. She's been living disguised as Astrid. Astrid was killed on Earth, not Amira. She is on her way to explain everything to her parents. I just want to be with Abishai. He's Amira's son. You must let me through. I have to be with him!" Dang it. I'm crying again. I thought I was all cried out.

He lets me go, and now he looks like he is going to cry. "Our Princess is alive?"

Devon and I take this opportunity to push past him and into the room. The team has taken off Abishai's bandage and are cleaning him up. Devon steps up beside me. Devon sees all the blood and looks a little queasy. I smile at him, "What? Don't like the sight of blood? Imagine that. Big, tough Devon."

Devon has gone white as a sheet. "Yeah. Ha-ha, real funny. Anyway, I need to go down to the shuttle and contact our parents anyway. I can smooth things over for us. You know, for taking off at graduation, being gone for so long, and now ending up on this habitat ship. You'll be okay here?" He's trying to smile despite the queasiness.

I give him a quick hug, "Yes, Devon I'll be fine. That's a great idea, in all this craziness I lost track of time. Mom is probably worried sick about me. Thank you."

He walks out the door, looking relieved. I step over to Abishai and hold his good hand. The nurses are all busy around us.

Someone taps me on my shoulder, to get my attention. "What happened here young lady? Why is this boy dehydrated and his arm all slashed up? Is he in some sort of trouble?" I look up to find a young doctor, tall, with a dark, chiseled face that unexpectedly belongs to a deep bass voice. His eyes are so dark they look black, and right now, angry.

I shrug away from his hand. "Do you know who this boy is? Didn't the other doctor tell you?" I place both my hands on Abishai's arm protectively and step as close as I can get to him.

Angry Eyes shakes his head. "No, just that he came from the shuttle that just left Dr. Kincaid's habitat ship. The very habitat ship that just had an explosion aboard." His words come out sharp as knives.

I stand my ground, even though I must admit I'm a bit intimidated by this guy. "This is Abishai Kincaid. His mother is Amira, who is upstairs talking to her parents." I'm shaking. I will not be separated from Abishai.

"That is a lie. Princess Amira died years ago on Earth."

I sigh. "I know it's all confusing, but I promise you I'm telling the truth. When Amira is done talking to her parents, she'll be down here to check on Abishai, and she expects him to be alive and well." I make sure to keep direct eye contact with him so he'll know I'm serious. I wonder how many times I'm going to have to explain this.

"Well, of course we will take care of him, no matter who he is. I will verify your story later. For now though, tell me how he got such a nasty cut on his arm and why he is dehydrated and starving."

He hasn't tried to remove me from the room, so I relax a little and answer him. "When Amira and I rescued him from his father's ship, he was locked in a storage room. He wasn't eating or drinking very much at all. He's lost a lot of weight since I last saw him a few weeks ago." Abishai starts thrashing around a bit, so I help the nurses hold down his arms. I look back up to Doctor Angry Eyes and continue.

"The arm is my fault. Dr. Kincaid had installed a detonation device in his arm. It was rigged to explode in Abishai's body if he were ever to leave the floor where he was being held captive. So I had to remove it, in order to get him out of there. All I had was alcohol and a steak knife. We were in a kitchen, not a med ward. Is he going to be all right? Did I cause permanent damage?" I'm crying now, scared for Abishai and the damage I might have caused.

Now Doctor Angry Eyes looks even angrier. Great. Now I've done it. He starts ordering nurses around in his native tongue. I'm surprised when one of the nurses quickly puts a gown and mask on me.

"What's wrong doctor? What did I say?" I feel lost, but grateful at the same time that they're not forcing me out of the room. I wish Abishai would wake up, so this whole nightmare would be over.

"That cretin! That lunatic!" Doctor Angry Eyes is yelling now, but I don't think he's mad at me this time. He looks at the cut in Abishai's arm. "That capsule that was implanted in his arm was my design! Dr. Kincaid said he needed a way to deliver doses of medicine to one of his senior staff. He told me that he had some strange type of disease from the Polymer Bacteria on Earth. I designed the capsule and sold it to him."

My mouth drops open. I guess I shouldn't be surprised how many lies Dr. Kincaid is capable of, but this is pretty low, even for him. "But you didn't know what Dr. Kincaid really was planning. It's not your fault. Dr. Kincaid has lied to many people."

He shakes his head. "You don't understand. It was designed to deliver a slow dose. We must treat Abishai for whatever kind of poison Dr. Kincaid added, besides the explosive."

"What? So is that why he wasn't hungry and why he's still so sick? Because he was being poisoned as well? You can fix him then, right? I can't lose him!" I'm very close to being totally hysterical now. "And we need to tell Amira at once!"

The doctor nods at one of the nurses who rushes out of the room. They poke all sorts of needles into Abishai and start dripping different meds into him. The doctor skillfully sutures up Abishai's arm and puts a clean dressing on it.

He frowns as he looks at the readouts coming from the many monitors around Abishai. "What is your name again, and how do you know this boy?"

"My name is Kaci. It's a long story how we met and an even longer one on how I found his mom. But in a nutshell, I crashed on Earth, got radiation poisoning from leaking nuclear weapons, then spent days recovering at the Compound with Abishai. Then..."

"Wait! Go back! You and Abishai were both exposed to radiation? When? For how long? What kind of treatment?" He suddenly closes the space between us and is looming directly over me.

Crap, he's tall. "Ummm...well it was about three or four weeks ago. Dr. Kincaid put us in a radiation chamber for several hours. It took us about two days to get our strength back. Why is that important now?"

"Yes! That is good! The lingering effects of the radiation treatment probably slowed down the spread of the toxin in his body. It will give us time to identify it and come up with the right treatment." He smiles now for the first time since I stepped in this room. I almost think I liked him angry better. It doesn't look like he has had much practice smiling.

I hear a commotion behind me. "Kaci! My goodness now what is wrong?" Amira rushes into the room, followed by a whole crowd of people dressed in colorful, flowing robes.

She grabs me and hugs me, while keeping Abishai in her sight at the same time.

I quickly explain to her what the doctor has just told me. Abishai stirs next to us. His color looks much better, and there is life behind his wonderful green eyes again. He is staring at me, smiling. In a weak voice he says, "I thought it was just a dream. Your hair, finally getting out of that storage room. But you really are here." I lean down and kiss him gently on his lips. My heart is bursting, so full of relief and love for this boy.

He turns his head the other way and looks at Amira. "Mom? Kaci tried to tell me you were still alive, but I still was not sure..."

"Yes, Abishai, I am here. You are aboard our family's ship, Habitat Mozambique. Your grandma and grandpa are here too. You are safe now, Robert cannot hurt you anymore." She is crying and wiping her nose as she steps back to allow her mom, the Queen of Mozambique, to come close to Abishai. I step back as well to allow Abishai to spend a few minutes with the family he has never known. I make my way through the crowd to the other side with Amira.

"How did it go telling them, Amira? They look pretty happy to see you and Abishai."

"Yes, they always suspected Robert of being untruthful. They held out hope to one day see me again." I put my arm around her and rest my head on her shoulder, as she cries. "They welcomed me back and are very happy to know I have a son, an heir to the throne. Traditions run deep in our culture. They will do whatever is necessary to keep Abishai safe from Robert. We have already recorded a message to the Council detailing everything Robert has done. We then sent a message to Robert letting him know that if he doesn't drop out of the Council and leave us alone, we will release the message to the whole holo vid network."

"Really? After all he's done? That is all you're going to do to him? Threaten him? I mean, look at what he has done to Abishai."

Amira smoothes down my hair and smiles down at me. "I know child, but we are a peaceful people. We believe without my family's money and the power that the Council gave him, that Robert will not be able to harm anyone ever again. He will have no power left. Besides, what better way to keep an eye on your enemy? In plain sight. As a businessman he will retain a seat on the Council, but he will not have a vote. Without my money, he will not be able to use bribery to increase his power."

"I guess you're right, Amira. I just hope they keep a close eye on him. Surely he will retain supporters for his role in saving Earth." Something doesn't sit right with me. I'm missing something important here, and my foggy brain isn't cooperating.

"Yes, he does have many supporters. His Project has been successful and will allow humanity to one day return to this solar system. Another good reason to keep this as quiet as possible; allow him to have the illusion of power. Otherwise it may look like we are going after the man who saved Earth. You know how influential the media vids are. He would have more support if we try to harm him publicly."

"Yes, I understand, but I don't like it." Amira's parents leave in a flurry of guards, so I return to Abishai's side.

I carefully grasp his hand around all the tubes and ask him, "How are you feeling, Abishai?"

"Been better." He gives me a weak smile and looks around the room. "That was quite overwhelming. I go from having just a crazy father, who was never really there for me, to a whole big family. They are all so nice, it will just take time getting used to. And I think some sleep might help me deal with it all." He squeezes my hand as he yawns. He looks into my eyes and pleads, "Please do not go away again, okay, Kaci?"

"I won't Abishai. I'm not going anywhere. I'll be right here when you wake up." I look up and see a nurse glaring at me. "I'll stay with him." I return her glare and then turn my focus back to Abishai. "Just get rest now. I'm right here, and when you wake up, we can catch up on all the crazy stuff that has happened to us since Earth." I carefully ease myself next to him on the bed.

Amira comes up beside me and whispers, "I will arrange for more comfortable accommodations for you, Kaci, here with Abishai. There will also be guards right outside the door. Looks like you could use some rest too." She kisses the top of my head and then Abishai's and walks out of the room.

After a few minutes, the nurse comes back in pushing another bed. She places it right next to Abishai's. I can tell she's still irked that I'm here, but Amira must have set her straight. She also leaves me a meal and clean clothes. I'm very grateful and make sure to tell her so.

I eat while Abishai falls asleep. I then peek out the door to make sure the guards really are still there. Relieved and feeling a bit safer, I head to the attached bathroom and take a quick shower. I feel much better now that I am clean and all the makeup is off. I like the reactions I get with all the makeup, but that wasn't me. Abishai likes me just the way I am, so I don't need it. Of course the blond hair will have to stay for a while longer. I put on clean clothes and tie my hair up in a ponytail.

I quietly settle down in the bed next to Abishai and fall asleep holding his hand. It's wonderful having him back and not having to worry about our safety.

CHAPTER 29

Nuclear Threat

I wake suddenly to an alarm going off. I sit up groggily and brace for another emergency. What is it this time? I have no idea how long I've slept. I look over at Abishai and see he's laughing at me. "What? Are we under attack? Why on Saturn's spot are you laughing?"

He leans close to me, now mostly on my bed. "It's all right, Kaci, relax. The alarms are just my monitors. I woke up confused too and forgot where I was. Then when I saw you laying there asleep, I tried to get up to be closer to you. I guess I pulled out some tubes and things."

"Then why are you laughing?" Good grief. My heart is racing, and those stupid alarms have given me an instant headache.

"Because you were ready to protect me, even half asleep, weren't you?" He points out that I have come to a fighting crouch on the hospital bed.

I settle back down on the bed. "You shouldn't laugh, or maybe next time I won't save you." My temper dissipates quickly as a flock of nurses come rushing in.

Abishai is still grinning at me, as the nurses work to connect all the tubes and wires he's pulled out. Several times he is reprimanded for trying to get up. Good. He can feel their wrath now.

They get him hooked back up, and I ease myself onto his bed, cuddling in next to him. He strokes my hair with his good arm, and I concentrate on his heartbeat and the steady in and out of his breathing.

"I was so worried I lost you forever, Kaci. I did not know if my father had killed you. I assumed all those years ago he had killed my mom, so I knew he was capable of it. Maybe I was wrong that he would go that far."

I shake my head. "No, you weren't wrong. He did kill Astrid, your mom's attendant and best friend, in order to make sure your mom didn't take you. She had to take Astrid's identity all these years to stay safe from him."

We lay there for hours talking about everything that had happened since we last saw each other on Earth. I learn that his father tried desperately to get him to go along with his plan; bribing him, threatening him. With Abishai's stubborn refusals, Dr. Kincaid finally told him I was dead. Dr. Kincaid thought that would make Abishai give in and join him, but it had the opposite effect. Abishai withdrew into himself and even several times tried to sabotage Dr. Kincaid's ship. So

Dr. Kincaid had Caleb imprison Abishai. The explosive implant was the last step in Dr. Kincaid's paranoia. Afraid, and rightly so, that Abishai would try to escape, he had the implant surgically placed into his arm.

"Abishai, do you think he realized the toxins would leak into your system? They would've eventually killed you." I shudder thinking what would've happened to Abishai if we hadn't gotten him out of there.

"Yes, I think he did, Kaci. He was so angry with me for defying him. When he failed to mold me into his perfect little robot son, he locked me away so that he would not be reminded of his failure. I think the slow death from the toxin, somehow distanced himself from my death. He could then pretend he was not responsible."

"Oh, Abishai. I'm so sorry we didn't come for you sooner. I tried thinking of ways to get you out. Even Devon came up with a few plans." I turn and study Abishai's face. I wonder if he resents me for not coming for him, or that maybe I should have tried to fight harder, when I was still on Earth.

"Kaci, I did not want you to risk yourself for me. I could not have lived with myself if you got hurt or killed, trying to rescue me." He plays with my hair, smoothing the whips that are escaping from my ponytail. "Besides if you did not wait this long, you might not have met my mom, and you would not have this fantastic hair color." He kisses me on the nose and laughs.

"Very funny. So you prefer me as a blonde?" I prop myself up on an elbow, so I can look directly at him.

"No, you know I am just teasing, Kaci. When I first saw you, I almost did not even recognize you." He kisses me firmly on the lips, and I forget everything we were just talking about. It's nice just being here with him.

Amira comes running in, startling us both. She rushes over to us.

"What is the matter, Mom? What has happened?"

"It's Robert. He is not accepting our compromise. He will not give up his power, and he says he is going to use his nuclear weapons on the Council ship." She is breathless from running.

A tingle goes down my spine. There is something more to this. "Amira. What does he want in order to call off the nukes?"

She looks at me and then at Abishai. Anger instantly flushes through my body. "Abishai? He wants Abishai? He cannot have him! I won't let Abishai go again. And besides, why does he want Abishai now? How does that help him?"

"Abishai is the heir to two kingdoms now. Mozambique and Botswana have combined leadership. Botswana is without an heir, so we are stronger together, with Abishai. If Robert has Abishai, he has their power as well." She is crying now, stroking Abishai's arm. Her personal guards and attendants have finally caught up with her and wait—out of breath—at the door.

Devon is also making his way past the crowd. He heads over to me. "Kaci, I just heard about Dr. Kincaid. His ship is on its way here."

"Devon, thank goodness you're still here. I thought command would order you back."

"They tried making me come back, but I requested leave for a while. Our parents are not too happy with us, so I really didn't want to go back and face them quite yet, anyway. Your mom especially seems to blame me for getting you in such trouble. Guess she doesn't know you that well, huh?" He's grinning. "Command denied my request for leave, but they did give me orders to stay aboard Mozambique to help with security. For now." He looks very satisfied with himself. He must have loved having his father give in to him that way. Looks like he might have a future in politics, after all.

"Good, I'm glad you're here Devon." I climb down from the bed. "Do you know why Dr. Kincaid is on his way here? And are you confident you were successful with our other little contingency plan on Dr. Kincaid's ship?"

"Yes, I heard he wants his power back. And Abishai. And yes, I did take care of it. Of course I did." He puffs out his chest, and I just have to roll my eyes at him.

I turn to Amira. "Who is in charge of this ship? We need to talk to them, now."

"The Captain is on the bridge, trying to figure out what to do about Dr. Kincaid's ship. You know these habitat ships aren't built for fighting. We have some shielding, but not strong enough to protect us from nuclear weapons. What do you mean about a contingency plan? What did you two do over there?" She looks between Devon and me.

"Take us to the Captain, Amira. I have an idea. I'll tell you on the way there." My training is kicking in, along with my stubbornness. I will not allow Dr. Kincaid to take Abishai away again.

Amira looks doubtful. "Kaci, I know you have accomplished some amazing things in the last few months, and we have been through a lot just in the last couple of days, but these are nuclear weapons we are talking about."

I walk over to her and grab her hands in mine. "Amira, you need to trust me. Devon and I need to get to the main comm console before I can tell if my plan is going to work. We need to hurry."

"I'm coming with you." Abishai says behind us, as he is making one of the nurses disconnect him from the machines.

"Abishai! No, you need to stay here and rest. Your body has been horribly traumatized." I go over to him and place my hands on his chest, trying to look stern.

He takes my hands in his and he leans in to kiss me. "Kaci, I will be fine. They…" He points at the nurses. "…can hover over me on the bridge as well as here. Besides, I am the ruling heir, and I can help you."

I sigh deeply. He's right. "Fine. We don't have time to argue." I turn to the nurses, "Make sure he stays alive. Take whatever you need to the bridge." I put my arm around his waist, helping him off the bed and turn to Devon. "Let's go. I hope this works." I smile as I walk past him and then realize we are still blocked in by Amira and her guards. They don't move.

"Amira?" I look directly into her eyes, pleading. "Please, Amira. You have trusted me this far. We still need to protect Abishai and all the people on this habitat. You know he won't have qualms about killing everyone. Devon and I have a plan. We have always suspected that Dr. Kincaid wouldn't go along with any kind of peaceful deal. You need to trust me."

Abishai speaks up weakly. "Mom, I trust her completely. Devon, too. You have trusted them before. Please, let us go."

Amira surprises me by stepping close and giving me a bear hug. I had expected more argument. "All right, child. Let's go then. I hope this plan of yours works better than your plans to stay out of trouble." She smiles and lets me go.

We reach the bridge amongst a flurry of activity. It's a large room, with two levels. The entire front wall is a view screen showing the approach of Dr. Kincaid's ship. There are people in uniforms running in and out of the room, pushing buttons, or staring at view screens. I settle Abishai down in a chair, in the middle of the room next to the metal railing that looks over the lower bridge. The nurses do their thing to make him comfortable.

Devon and I step toward the main comm. Two guards step forward to block our path. We look over at Amira.

She waves her hand. "Let them go. This is Kaci Lee and Devon Durrant. They were aboard Rob – Dr. Kincaid's ship. Captain?" Amira looks over at a tall, imposing man that has stepped up beside her. His graying hair is neatly clipped, and he is in full dress uniform. He steps over to where we stand. He is so tall and so close, that I have to look up, craning my neck. Are all the men here this tall? He has a lot of medals and pins on his uniform and a very serious expression on his face. I focus on a spot just past his shoulder, trying hard not to look nervous.

"So, Kaci. You think with four years experience in the Space Corps, that you know enough to eliminate this big of a threat? Nuclear weapons. You're only seventeen years old!"

I gear up for a colorful retort, when Abishai speaks up behind me. "Captain. I too, am only seventeen years old, but here I am, the heir and ruler over two countries. Our culture usually values its youth, does it not?" Abishai is now standing, shoulders square, keeping unwavering eye contact with the Captain. He has his hands behind his back, to hide his trembling. I can tell it is taking a lot of effort to just stand upright. The nurses around him look nervous. Everyone on the bridge is silent, holding their collective breaths.

Without changing his expression, the Captain turns to me. "Fine. Kaci, proceed with your plan, but you will tell me everything I need to know."

"Thank you." I turn quickly and step over to the console, where Devon is already working.

He points to the screen in front of him. "Here it is, Kaci. I embedded it in the shuttle's life support programming."

"Genius, Devon! What does it say?"

The Captain steps up beside us. "What are you two looking at?"

Devon answers, without looking up. "While Kaci and Amira were busy rescuing Abishai, I was working on a backup plan. When Kaci and Abishai were caught aboard the armed ship on Earth, they had disarmed five of the six nuclear weapons Dr. Kincaid has. They hid the uranium components behind a console. I snuck in and found the box. No one had discovered it yet. I also found and removed the sixth weapon's uranium and hid all of it safely in empty oxygen tanks on our shuttle." He turns to the officers standing behind us. They are staring at Devon like he has grown a second head. "Don't worry, I already had your chief engineer remove it and place it somewhere safe." Devon motioned to a stocky man near the back of the room. "Amira, as the chief engineer of the Botswana, of course knew who I could trust over here." The man smiles and nods at Devon in acknowledgment. The officers look relieved.

Devon turns back and faces the Captain. "So, then I hid a security patch in the programming of the shuttle, as Amira had taught me. It allows us to patch into Dr. Kincaid's main computer systems. In a few minutes, we should be able to bring it online. We will be able to tell if Dr. Kincaid has discovered the deactivated nukes and if there are any more we don't know about."

"That is quite impressive, Devon. You learned all that from the Princess?" We all whirl around at the very familiar voice. In the doorway is Commander Durrant, Devon's father and Commander of the Migration. Crap. My palms start sweating. The only person with more power and thus scarier than Dr. Kincaid is the commander. And he doesn't look happy.

"Uh, yes sir. No, sir!" Devon looks a bit uneasy. I bet he didn't think he would have to face his father so soon. I relax a bit knowing that I'm not the only one nervous all of a sudden.

The Captain walks up to the Commander and greets him, nervously, "Welcome to Habitat Ship Mozambique, Commander. It is an honor to have you aboard. I apologize for not having a welcoming committee awaiting you. If I had known you were coming..."

The Commander holds up his hand. "That would defeat the purpose of a surprise visit then, would it not?" The Commander's voice and body language are stern, but the corners of his eyes are smiling. The Captain's complexion has paled a bit, and he steps back.

Having known this man practically my whole life, I know that he is baiting the Captain. He likes people to be nervous and unbalanced around him. I decide to intervene to save the Captain from more embarrassment.

I step forward. "It's okay, Captain. The Commander is here to make a surprise appearance on Devon and me, not you. I tend to be on the Commander's radar a lot." I smile at the Captain and hope that my hunch is right.

The Commander is silent at first, staring me down. Then he startles all of us, as he starts laughing. "Yes, Kaci. As usual you have caught my attention, and I have come see what kind of trouble you—and this time my son—have gotten into. Seems you have outdone yourself this time." He nods to the view screen.

I wish I could wipe the smug look off of his face. I clench my hands into fists, sinking my nails into my palms, to keep myself calm.

Devon steps over next to me. "Sir, if I could interrupt. Dr. Kincaid is less than twenty minutes away, and I need Kaci to help me here." Devon to the rescue, again.

I don't wait for an answer from the Commander. We turn and step back over to the console. I'm confident they won't stop us. Even though the Commander is itching to see me fail, he is also Devon's father, which of course is why Devon gets away with so much on Jupiter Station. I shake my head at the irony of all this.

I look over the data that Devon has pulled up on the screen. I smile at the readouts and look at Devon. He smiles back, confirming that I have read the information correctly. I turn back to the Commander. "The information has confirmed that the nukes Abishai and I deactivated, are still deactivated. So is the one Devon took care of, and they don't know about it yet. More importantly, there are no other nukes aboard. The scan shows that there aren't any traces of uranium or plutonium on board any of his ships. He has no way to create another nuclear weapon."

Amira rushes over and grabs Devon and me into another one of her crushing hugs. "Good work, you two!" She releases us and turns to the comm console. "Now, it is my turn. Time I talk to Robert and end this."

CHAPTER 30

Psychotic Break

Amira adjusts the comm, hailing the other ship and requests to talk to Dr. Kincaid himself. After a few minutes, Dr. Kincaid comes on the front display, looking very tired and rumpled. His hair is sticking out in all directions, and his white lab coat is stained and wrinkled.

"Yes. What is it? What is your answer to my demands?" His eyes are trying to focus, scanning the faces on our bridge. Amira clears her throat loudly, and his eyes lock onto her.

"Amira?"

"Yes, Robert. I am still quite alive. Sorry to disappoint you. I'm not going to hide from you anymore. You cannot control me, and you cannot have Abishai. So stand your weapons down."

"This is impossible." He runs his hands through his hair, as he tries to gather his thoughts. I can see where Abishai gets that habit from.

He suddenly looks up, his eyes darting from side to side. He stops on the Commander and then goes back to Amira. "This is... Well, I am so glad to see you. I have been looking for you all these years. Amira, my wife." The last sentence is spoken with a grating, possessive voice. Does he really think that's going to work?

"You can drop the act, Robert. Everyone here on this bridge knows the truth. How you forced me off Earth, away from my son. How you killed my best friend Astrid, to keep me quiet." Amira is trembling, trying to control her temper.

Dr. Kincaid spits out, "You are still my wife! Give me back my son!"

"I filed for divorce already with the Council, Robert. It should be final today. The Council granted it right after you threatened us with nuclear weapons. Reasons of insanity." She looks conflicted between anger and pity for this man she once loved.

Before he can say anything, Amira continues in a calmer voice, "It didn't have to go this way. You could have met our compromise. You could have kept a seat on the Council and worked alongside us."

Dr. Kincaid brings his hands down hard on the console in front of him. "No! You want to take all my power. I created the Eugenesis Project! I saved Earth's future! I should be in charge of the Migration! Me!" He has to stop to take a few breaths. "And I still will be. I see the Commander has graced us with his presence." Dr. Kincaid drills his gaze on the Commander. "First of all, you will send over Abishai.

And I won't need his money, I have plenty of gold. Then you will transfer all authority to me. You will make me Commander over the Migration!"

The Commander starts to reply, but Abishai steps forward. He stands next to me, leaning heavily on me for support. "No, Father. I will not go with you, ever. My home is here. I will not allow you to hurt me, my family, or my friends."

"I don't care what you say, you will obey me!" Dr. Kincaid's voice has risen into a high pitched, desperate tone. He grabs Caleb, who is standing behind him, and drags him over to a console to the side. "Caleb here has already armed the nuclear weapons. We have them aimed at Habitat ships Botswana, Mozambique, and of course your precious Jupiter Station. You will all do as I ask, or we will launch the weapons. In a matter of seconds hundreds of thousands of people will be dead! You don't want to be responsible for all their deaths, do you?" Caleb is pale and looks like he's going to puke. I almost feel sorry for him. Almost.

Amira tells Dr. Kincaid calmly, "You can't do that Robert."

"Yes, I can! And I will!"

"No, you can't. Literally. Kaci, Devon, and Abishai have disarmed your weapons. They are useless." She is fiercely staring at him.

"Impossible! You're bluffing! What would you know? There is no way those kids have done anything!" He glances over at Caleb, who is typing furiously at the console. "Caleb! Fire one of the nukes at the Botswana ship! That'll show them I am serious!"

Caleb nervously answers, "Sir, they are right. The sensors say the nukes are ready, but they won't arm."

A sound like some sort of wounded animal comes from Dr. Kincaid, and in a fury he launches himself at Caleb. I wince as he strikes Caleb down. Dr. Kincaid has moved out of the range of the video, but we still can hear him yelling and swearing. It sounds like he has gone from hitting Caleb, to destroying all the computer consoles in his rage. I look at the Commander. He just shrugs his shoulders. Great. Real helpful. But I guess there really isn't anything we can do at this point.

I look over at Amira and she has tears in her eyes. I reach out and squeeze her hand. Abishai tightens his grip around my waist. It must be hard to see someone they once loved go crazy like this. We all knew he was dangerous and a bit mental, but he has definitely gone off the deep end now. There isn't anything else we can do for him.

Suddenly, the wall screen goes black. We have been disconnected. Amira tries to get him back, but there is no response. We switch the vid display in time to see his ship start to move. What will he do, ram into us? Could we get away in time? I look around and see that everyone has frozen, waiting to see what will happen.

Dr. Kincaid's ship starts picking up speed, and then we notice that he is actually heading away from us. Everyone starts clapping and cheering. Relief is felt throughout the whole bridge.

I don't cheer and neither does Abishai or Amira. We realize he is heading the opposite direction of the Migration. Away from us, away from all of humanity.

Abishai slides down to the floor, pulling me with him. I wrap my arms around him and we just lean against each other. Eventually, I allow the nurses to help him back down to his room. After he is hooked back up to the machines, I climb back up on the edge of his bed. Amira is sitting on my bed. The Commander and Devon are on the other side of the room, talking quietly. We are all exhausted, mentally and physically.

The Commander comes over to us. "We have tracked Dr. Kincaid on long range sensors. He continues on his course past Earth." We nod. "I don't know how he plans on surviving out there alone."

None of us has a response to that. His warped mind has condemned his crew to a slow death, as they will eventually run out of supplies. Unless they come back and join the Migration, but I don't see Dr. Kincaid doing that peacefully.

The Commander continues, "Well, I need to get back to the Council to explain all this." He turns to Devon. "I am proud of you son. You have done well, and you helped Kaci and Abishai and the Mozambique without asking for anything in return. You have matured a lot in the last few months." He gives a rare smile to Devon, as Devon beams at his father. Then the Commander turns to Abishai and me. "I want to thank you two as well, for your role in everything that has happened over the last few weeks. I'm sure the Council will be pleased." The Commander nods to Amira, and he and Devon both walk out of the room, followed by all of the officers and delegates from Mozambique and Botswana.

It takes a few weeks for Abishai to regain his strength and for my mom to stop being angry at me. When things have finally settled down, the first thing I do is take Abishai out in my Scout ship.

Abishai and I enjoy the time alone and the quietness and comfort of space and the stars. As the stars slide by, we hold hands and talk about our future. Almost like a real date.

"Do you think we will reach New Earth in our lifetime, Kaci?"

I smile. "I don't know. The engineers are always working on improving our space drives. Maybe someday they will discover a way to get us there faster. In the meantime, I have everything I need."

He squeezes my hand. "Kaci, I want to be wherever you are. I love you, and I do not want to be away from you ever again. What I plan to do the rest of my life, is love you with all of my heart. I bet I could even one day learn to fly this ship, despite a lack of certain natural aptitudes." Abishai winks at me, with a mischievous look in his shining emerald green eyes.

I sigh contently. "I love you too, Abishai, but you still can't fly my ship. I remember how badly you fly." I laugh and program the ship to return home. I lean over and give Abishai a kiss, closing my eyes to enjoy the sensation of flying through space next to the love of my life.

The End

ACKNOWLEDGMENTS

Writing is such a fun and fantastic journey and I'm blessed by all the people I've met.

Thanks to all the readers for coming along on this journey with me. I hope you enjoy the other books in this series as well!

You can find me at:
http://www.HeatherLeeDyer.com
Twitter: @HeatherLeeDyer_
Facebook: https://www.facebook.com/heatherleedyer/
Instagram: kunadyers

Made in the USA
San Bernardino, CA
08 June 2017